LAURIE PAIGE
MAKE WAY FOR BABIES!

Silhouette ®

SPECIAL EDITION ®

Published by Silhouette Books
America's Publisher of Contemporary Romance

For William.
Welcome to the family!

Special thanks and acknowledgment are given to Laurie Paige for her contribution to the So Many Babies series.

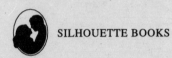 SILHOUETTE BOOKS

ISBN 0-373-24317-0

MAKE WAY FOR BABIES!

Visit Silhouette at www.eHarlequin.com

Printed in U.S.A.

SO MANY BABIES

Four heart-tugging stories about the littlest matchmakers—as they find their way through the Buttonwood Baby Clinic and into a family's welcoming arms!

THE BABY LEGACY by Pamela Toth
Special Edition #1299 On sale January 2000

When an anonymous sperm donor tries to withdraw his "contribution," he learns a beautiful woman is eight months pregnant—with *his* child!

WHO'S THAT BABY? by Diana Whitney
Special Edition #1305 On sale February 2000

A handsome Native American lawyer finds a baby on his doorstep—and more than he bargains for with an irresistible pediatrician who has more than medicine on her mind!

MILLIONAIRE'S INSTANT BABY
by Allison Leigh
Special Edition #1312 On sale March 2000

Pretend to be married to a millionaire "husband"? It seemed an easy way for this struggling single mom to earn a trust fund for her newborn. But she never thought she'd fall for her make-believe spouse....

MAKE WAY FOR BABIES! by Laurie Paige
Special Edition #1317 On sale April 2000

All she needed was a helping hand with her infant twins—until her former brother-in-law stepped up to play "daddy," and stepped right into her heart.

Dear Reader,

With spring in the air, there's no better way to herald the season and continue to celebrate Silhouette's 20th Anniversary year than with an exhilarating month of romance from Special Edition!

Kicking off a great lineup is *Beginning with Baby,* a heartwarming THAT'S MY BABY! story by rising star Christie Ridgway. Longtime Special Edition favorite Susan Mallery turns up the heat in *The Sheik's Kidnapped Bride,* the first book in her new DESERT ROGUES series. And popular author Laurie Paige wraps up the SO MANY BABIES miniseries with *Make Way for Babies!,* a poignant reunion romance in which a set of newborn twins unwittingly plays Cupid!

Beloved author Gina Wilkins weaves a sensuous modern love story about two career-minded people who are unexpectedly swept away by desire in *Surprise Partners.* In *Her Wildest Wedding Dreams* from veteran author Celeste Hamilton, a sheltered woman finds the passion of a lifetime in a rugged rancher's arms. And finally, Carol Finch brings every woman's fantasy to life with an irresistible millionaire hero in her compelling novel *Soul Mates.*

It's a gripping month of reading in Special Edition. Enjoy!

All the best,

Karen Taylor Richman
Senior Editor

Please address questions and book requests to:
Silhouette Reader Service
U.S.: 3010 Walden Ave., P.O. Box 1325, Buffalo, NY 14269
Canadian: P.O. Box 609, Fort Erie, Ont. L2A 5X3

LAURIE PAIGE

says, "One of the nicest things about writing romances is researching locales, careers and ideas. In the interest of authenticity, most writers will try anything...once." Along with her writing adventures, Laurie has been a NASA engineer, a past president of the Romance Writers of America (twice!), a mother and a grandmother (twice, also!). She was twice a Romance Writers of America RITA Award finalist for Best Traditional Romance, and has won awards from *Romantic Times Magazine* for Best Silhouette Special Edition and Best Silhouette. She has also been presented with *Affaire de Coeur*'s Readers' Choice Silver Pen Award for Favorite Contemporary Author. Recently resettled in Northern California, Laurie is looking forward to whatever experiences her next novel will send her on.

IT'S OUR 20th ANNIVERSARY!
We'll be celebrating all year,
Continuing with these fabulous titles,
On sale in April 2000.

Romance

#1438 Carried Away
Kasey Michaels/Joan Hohl

#1439 An Eligible Stranger
Tracy Sinclair

#1440 A Royal Marriage
Cara Colter

#1441 His Wild Young Bride
Donna Clayton

#1442 At the Billionaire's Bidding
Myrna Mackenzie

#1443 The Marriage Badge
Sharon De Vita

Desire

#1285 Last Dance
Cait London

#1286 Night Music
BJ James

#1287 Seduction, Cowboy Style
Anne Marie Winston

#1288 The Barons of Texas: Jill
Fayrene Preston

#1289 Her Baby's Father
Katherine Garbera

#1290 Callan's Proposition
Barbara McCauley

Intimate Moments

#997 The Wildes of Wyoming—Hazard
Ruth Langan

#998 Daddy by Choice
Paula Detmer Riggs

#999 The Harder They Fall
Merline Lovelace

#1000 Angel Meets the Badman
Maggie Shayne

#1001 Cinderella and the Spy
Sally Tyler Hayes

#1002 Safe in His Arms
Christine Scott

Special Edition

#1315 Beginning with Baby
Christie Ridgway

#1316 The Sheik's Kidnapped Bride
Susan Mallery

#1317 Make Way for Babies!
Laurie Paige

#1318 Surprise Partners
Gina Wilkins

#1319 Her Wildest Wedding Dreams
Celeste Hamilton

#1320 Soul Mates
Carol Finch

Chapter One

Spencer McBride parked in the lot at the Button-wood Baby Clinic with a feeling of unease. He'd found an odd message from his mom on his voice mail when he returned to the office shortly before five that afternoon.

Spence, honey, this is Mom. Come to the clinic ASAP. Something important has come up. Hurry!

As executive administrator of the clinic, Rose McBride was in charge of the business affairs there. Maybe some nutcase was threatening to sue the clinic. Or bomb it. Who knew what people would do nowadays?

However, her tone had indicated the matter was exciting rather than threatening. So maybe it wasn't bad news.

Stretching his shoulders and covering a yawn, he headed toward the attractive building. It had been a hard day. He'd spent most of it in court, arguing a case in which the judge had decided against his client in a mineral-lease claim.

The client wanted to appeal. Spence had advised the rancher that his chances of overturning the lease agreement signed by the previous owner were slim. The mining company wasn't going to give up a lucrative deal without a fight.

He smiled absently at the receptionist when he entered the clinic, skirted the information area and strode into his mother's office. The secretary, Marci Bonn, was locking up.

"Oh, hi. You're just in time," she said, adding to the sense of mystery surrounding the message.

Her bright smile indicated male-female interest. He ignored it as he had each time he'd been in the office during the few months since he'd moved back to Buttonwood and gone into law practice with Johnny Winterhawk, a friend from high-school days.

"Your mom said I was to bring you right down," Marci continued.

"She isn't in her office?"

"No. She's, uh, waiting somewhere else."

The smile grew more mysterious as she checked the lock on the file cabinet, grabbed her purse and dashed for the door. Spence gave an exasperated snort as he followed the young woman out of the office.

He hoped his mom wasn't on one of her matchmaking kicks. She'd been trying to tie him up with various women for years. At thirty-two, he was a confirmed bachelor.

Or maybe he just hadn't met the *one,* as his mom insisted.

The secretary led the way down one of the clinic's four main corridors, which smelled of cinnamon and…pizza, he decided. It was dinnertime. His stomach was reminding him he'd missed lunch.

"In there." She pointed toward a patient room, all the while beaming at him as if something momentous was happening, or was going to happen now that he was here. A chill of foreboding slid down his neck.

"My mom's in there?" he questioned, just to make sure they were on the same track. A new worry attacked him. "Is she okay?"

"She's fine. Go on in." Walking a couple of steps backward, Marci waved and smiled some more, then turned and retreated toward the reception area.

Totally mystified, Spence called "Thanks" and went into the room a bit cautiously, not sure what he would find. It wasn't his birthday or anything like that—

"Spence, you're just in time," his mom said, appearing at the door. She grabbed his arm and tugged him inside.

His first impression was one of lots of people. Four women, plus the usual hospital paraphernalia, were jammed into the small room. One female was a patient, in bed and quite obviously pregnant. And totally unknown to him.

He fell back a step, confused by the situation. The room felt crowded and filled with a complexity he couldn't describe. Perhaps this was a paternity case, and the young woman needed help. "Mom, maybe we'd better step outside—"

"Spence!" another female exclaimed, turning from the woman lying on the bed and leaning past his mother's shoulder to smile at him in delight.

A funny feeling raced over his skin, an electric tingle that started a thrum of response someplace deep inside him. He'd recognize that sexy bow-drawn-over-a-rusty-saw voice anywhere, anytime.

Ally Henderson McBride. His brother's widow.

Once she'd been his best friend. Years ago. Like his law partner, Ally belonged to high-school days and sweet memories of the past....

"What's happening?" he asked in a professional manner. Lawyers, like cops, ran into all kinds of situations. A person learned to take them in stride.

"This is a birthing room," a voice snapped with military precision as if his question had been the utmost in stupidity.

He recognized Maryanne Winters, who had graduated high school three years ahead of him. She'd gone into the army, then returned to Buttonwood as a nurse. He thought she should have been a drill sergeant.

"Your niece and nephew are about to be born," his mom told him, still holding his arm. "I'm glad you got here. I was afraid you were going to miss the big event.''

"Isn't it wonderful?" Ally added, throwing her own hundred-watt smile his way. "Here, let me introduce you to the birth mother, Taylor Fletcher. Taylor, this is Spence McBride, Rose's younger son. Jack's brother.''

For a second, Spence saw a shadow flash through Ally's eyes as she mentioned her deceased husband. Jack had been killed in a construction accident just before Christmas. It had been a hard time for all of them.

That was when he'd decided to move back to Buttonwood and take up Johnny's offer of a partnership. His mom had been so distraught after Jack's death, especially since it followed his dad's by less than a year.

"I'm glad…to meet you," the young woman on the bed welcomed him with a hitch in her voice.

"Glad to meet you, too." He didn't offer to shake hands. He wasn't sure of the protocol in this situation.

He had, of course, known about the twins and Ally's plans to adopt them, but never in his wildest dreams had he thought of being present when they were born. Whether Ally was the one having them or not, that honor belonged to her husband.

The birth mother couldn't have been more than eighteen or nineteen, twenty at the most. Her long blond hair was gathered at the back of her neck. Her face, pretty, young and very serious, was scrubbed clean of makeup. Something about her earnestness reminded him of Ally when she'd been eighteen and filled with plans for the future.

"We've decided to name the twins Hannah and Nicholas," Ally continued. "What do you think?"

Spence thought he should get the hell out of there. "Uh, that sounds fine. I'll, uh, wait in the hall or…or somewhere."

Anywhere but here!

Sweat broke out on his forehead. He couldn't believe his mom had meant him to come in here. The young woman was about to have a baby—no, two of them!

"Oh, don't you want to stay and welcome the babies?" Ally asked, her eyes wide as if shocked and hurt that he didn't want to participate.

During all the years he'd stayed away from his brother and his pretty sister-in-law, Spence had never forgotten those eyes. They were the brightest, clearest blue, with a darker blue encircling the lighter shade around the pupil. Her eyes and that rusty voice—they were the things he most remembered about her. And that she had been his best friend throughout their growing years, up until they graduated and went off to college…and their separate ways.

When he'd returned, Ally had been engaged to his brother. She and Jack were married that summer.

He'd gone off to law school in the autumn and never returned, except on short visits. He'd established a practice in Durango—close, but not too close, to his family.

"Well," he hedged, "I don't want to be in the way or make..." He tried to think of the young mother's name.

"Taylor," Ally supplied.

"Yeah. I don't want to make Taylor nervous."

"It's okay," the young woman said. "Jack was supposed to be here. It's okay if you stay."

Hell, he could hardly leave now. It would seem rude. Which was maybe the weirdest thought he'd ever had.

"If you're sure," he murmured, unable to think of a graceful exit line.

"It's time," Maryanne snapped. "Let's get the bed fixed and you in position."

Spence swallowed hard when he realized the crabby nurse was removing a panel from the bed, then helping Taylor into the birthing position. The fierce July heat seemed to penetrate the room and gather in his neck, ears and face.

He peered through the mini-blinds at the scene in the nearby park, trying to focus anywhere but the room where the sheets were being lifted and folded back and Taylor's knees were being exposed, rising above her mounded tummy.

Spence loosened his tie and opened a couple of buttons at his throat. He was having trouble breathing. He watched the kids playing in the park.

"Deep breaths," Maryanne ordered. "Slow and easy."

He forced himself to breathe deeply.

"The mother, not you," Maryanne said with scornful amusement.

"Right," he responded, as if this was old stuff to him. He risked a glance at the nurse. She folded a towel over the young mother's knees. His face felt like a furnace.

"Where's Dr. Parker?" Ally said, glancing past Spence toward the door.

"It's Friday night. He's probably on his way to his mountain cabin with some bimbo," Maryanne said, clearly indicating her opinion of the doctor's private life.

"Ohh," Taylor said and reached for Ally's hand.

"Is it time to pant?" Ally asked.

"I hope not," Maryanne said grimly. "I'll be back in a minute." She sailed out of the room, giving Spence a glare as she swept past.

Spence suppressed a need to tell her he was innocent. He wasn't the cause of the pregnancy, nor had he barged in uninvited. In fact, he'd rather not be there at all.

"There, darling," Ally crooned.

Spence's eyes were drawn to her. If a woman ever spoke to him in that tone he'd melt at her feet. It was caring and tender and filled with sweet encouragement. A chill ran down his spine, totally at odds with the furnace that glowed on his face.

He unbuttoned the cuffs of his white business shirt and rolled the sleeves up, glad that he'd tossed his jacket into the back seat of the car when he'd left the office.

The nurse returned in a minute. Claire Winterhawk, his partner's wife and a pediatrician, entered with her. As the sole male, he definitely felt out of place in the roomful of women. He tried to think of a reason to leave…immediately!

"Hi, Taylor, I'm Dr. Davis," Claire said. "I'm on call this evening, so I'll assist you in the birth. I'll be the twins' pediatrician, so this is exciting, getting to meet them first thing, huh?"

Spence breathed a silent sigh of relief. He felt better having a doctor on hand. Claire and Johnny had only been married a couple of months and had adopted a baby themselves. He'd taken over the final paperwork for them.

Johnny was handling the adoption of the twins for Ally. Which Spence thought was good. He didn't want to get too involved with his former best friend.

"Let's see how you're doing," Claire said jovially. She sat down on a stool between the young mother's legs.

Spence felt the heat rise in his face once more. He quickly glanced away. His gaze met Ally's. The world shifted; for a moment, he felt as if she saw into his soul and beyond, way back to the years when he'd been angry with her for marrying Jack, for not waiting for him.

Regret and surprise slammed through him. Where had that thought come from? He'd never asked her to wait.

"Get on the other side and take Taylor's hand," Ally ordered in gentle tones. "We'll help her breathe. She took Lamaze classes with Dr. Davis."

Help her breathe? Classes?

Spence felt he'd landed in another world where

they spoke the same language he did, but the words meant entirely different things. He went to where Ally had told him to stand, studiously keeping his eyes averted from what was happening at the other end of the raised hospital bed.

"Are you going to go by Davis or change to Winterhawk now that you've married Johnny?" his mother asked, peering over Ally's shoulder.

"I've decided to stay with Davis in my professional life. It's easier, since everyone in town knows me by that." Claire leaned forward. "Okay, get ready."

"Easy, easy," Ally murmured to Taylor.

"Let's hit it," Claire said as if encouraging a football team to play its best.

"Push," Maryanne said, doing things with spray bottles and towels.

Taylor groaned and pulled against his hand. Alarm spread through him at her expression. He couldn't tell if it was one of intense pain or intense concentration. Sweat trickled down his spine. He stared at a kid running across the park lawn, his mother hot on his trail. The mother captured the spunky toddler and led him back to the bench where she'd been sitting.

"Pant," Ally said and proceeded to do so.

She and Taylor panted in unison. Spence did, too, then realized what he was doing and tried to stop. He noted his mom also breathed with Taylor.

"Push!" Maryanne barked again as if the young mother had disobeyed a direct order.

Taylor pushed. Ally pushed. Rose pushed. And

Spence pushed. They panted. Sweat collected on their foreheads.

"Okay, relax," Claire said.

"Deep breaths," Maryanne commanded. They breathed.

Ally was aware of Spence across the narrow bed from her, his head inches away as they leaned over Taylor and helped her with the birthing. As everyone in the room relaxed, she spared him a sympathetic glance. She didn't recall ever seeing him blush, but now his face looked as if he had a good case of the measles. Her smile widened.

While they rested for the next big push, her thoughts turned introspective. She regretted that she would never be able to share this moment with her husband. She was barren. That was why she and Jack had been delighted when the chance came to adopt Taylor's children.

Tears burned her eyes as she recalled that Jack hadn't known they were having twins. He'd died shortly before Taylor had the checkup that revealed the two heartbeats. She took a careful breath and controlled her sorrow. This wasn't the place for it.

Now was the time for joy. She and Taylor had discussed the situation. She still wanted the babies, even though there were two and she was alone now. Taylor still wanted her to have them. The nineteen-year-old college student felt the children needed the secure home that Ally could afford and she couldn't. Both agreed Rose McBride would make a wonderful, doting grandmother, and Taylor could see the twins as often as her studies and workload would allow.

So it would all work out fine. She mentally crossed her fingers. She knew what happened to best-laid plans.

"Okay, here comes another one," Dr. Davis said.

Ally concentrated on Taylor and her breathing. At her left shoulder, Rose breathed with them, and across the bed, Spence unconsciously did, too.

Maryanne directed them. "Keep pushing. Okay, it's crowning."

Ally looked to see what this meant. She gulped and swallowed hard as she saw the very top of a head appear, a ridge running down the middle where the skull plates slid past each other so the baby could squeeze out. Her heart contracted in a mixture of excitement and deep emotion.

She glanced at Spence. He looked uneasy but stoic. For a moment, she was flooded with tenderness toward him. That was odd, but she was glad Rose had, for whatever strange reason, insisted he join them. Welcoming a new generation into the world was a momentous event for a family.

"Okay, once more," Claire said cheerfully. "You're doing wonderfully, Taylor."

"Thank you," Taylor said politely.

Ally met Spence's eyes and grinned. He gave her a searching glance. She sensed questions in him, but there wasn't time to ask what they were. "The baby," she said. "Here it comes."

The entire head appeared. Claire efficiently

cleared its nose and mouth. "One last big one, I think," she murmured after they'd rested a bit.

"Ohh," Ally and Rose and Taylor all chorused together when the baby was born, sliding smoothly into the doctor's waiting hands with one more push.

"Is the little darling here already?" another nurse crooned, bustling into the room, a baby blanket in hand. "Ah, a sweetheart of a girl," she said.

Ally recognized the woman as one of the pediatric nurses, Nell Hastings. A calm, gray-haired woman in her fifties, she took care of newborns with an ease that was guaranteed to soothe young parents. She dried the baby and wrapped her in another blanket, then proceeded to weigh and measure the child.

"Five pounds, seven ounces," she announced. "A very nice size for twins."

"No rest for the weary," Claire said to Taylor with an encouraging smile. "Ready for number two?"

Taylor barely had time to say yes before the contraction started and didn't let up. The team panted and pushed along with the mother. Nicholas came into the world as smoothly as his sister. He took one glance around the crowded room and howled. Startled, Hannah joined in.

"They're here," Ally said, tears starting in her eyes. "Taylor, they're here."

She and Taylor hugged and cried and kissed each other's cheeks while the nurse put wristbands on the infants, then weighed and measured the second one. "This big fellow is six pounds. I'm impressed," she told them.

Feeling a hand caressing her hair, Ally raised her head. Spence gave her an encouraging smile. His eyes looked a little misty, too.

"Oh, Spence, aren't they the most beautiful babies you ever saw?" she said.

He nodded and continued to stroke her hair in the gentlest manner.

She threw her arms around his neck and kissed him, all cautious thoughts fleeing in this moment of jubilation. She loved him. She loved Taylor. And Rose and Claire. Even the crabby nurse. And especially the twins, Hannah and Nicholas.

Sniffing, she drew back and pulled her emotions into order. "Sorry. I didn't mean to drown you two." She wiped tears off Spence's shirt and Taylor's forehead, then blotted Taylor's face with a washcloth. "You did just great," she assured the young woman.

"Did I?" Taylor said shakily. She looked from Ally to Spence to Rose. "Thanks for being here. It was just like having a real family—" She stopped as her lips trembled.

Rose patted her arm. "We *are* a real family, and you're a special part of it. Thank you for this wonderful gift."

"You'll want pictures before I take them to the warmers," the baby nurse said. She handed one infant to Ally. The other she plopped in Spence's arms. "Here, Daddy."

Ally couldn't help but laugh as Spence reacted

in typical surprised-bachelor horror. The child could have been a bomb ready to detonate instead of his nephew.

"I'm not the father," he hastily corrected. He carefully held the baby out in both hands. The nurse ignored his desperate expression.

"He's the uncle," Ally explained.

Rose grabbed a camera from her purse. "Hold Nicholas in the crook of your arm, Spence, the way Ally has Hannah."

Ally grinned when he looked worried and gingerly held the baby as directed. Rose snapped pictures like mad.

"Now Taylor with the babies," Ally requested. "Spence, put your hand over Taylor's on that side." She did the same and leaned close. "Lean down, Spence. And smile. This is a happy event."

After they had taken every possible combination of photo for the babies' album, the kind nurse whisked the little ones off to the warmer. Taylor yawned.

Ally was aware that Spence had played his part gallantly…after he got over the shock of being in on the birthing. She felt an enormous sense of pride about the whole event and everyone's part in it.

However, she was a tad embarrassed about the emotional kiss she'd plastered on him when he had caressed her in that gentle way. Poor bachelor uncle. This would be a day he wouldn't soon forget. Rose had some explaining to do to her handsome, and single, son.

* * *

Spence remained in the waiting room while the babies were bathed and put in a warmer—he imagined something like a chicken incubator with dozens of babies tucked into their little individual pockets. Ally had gone with the baby nurse to help with the twins while his mom stayed with Taylor.

In the nearby nurses' station, he heard two student nurses discussing someone. Rachel—another nurse, he surmised—was pregnant and due to deliver soon. They speculated on possible candidates for the father and mentioned Dr. Reid.

Spence was surprised. Dennis Reid was chief of staff at the clinic and sometimes a pain in the neck for Rose in her role as administrator. The man was nearly fifty, a tad old to be getting a woman pregnant out of wedlock.

He wondered if there was a paternity case in the offing, and knew he wasn't going to handle it if there was. His specialty was ranching cases, not personal problems. He and Johnny were contract attorneys.

He sipped the bitter coffee from the machine. Ugh. It was hard to take on an empty stomach. As if by way of a gentle reminder, his stomach growled.

"Yeah, yeah," he said.

Ally bustled into the room. "Hi. Talking to yourself? Better watch it. That's the second sign of senility."

"What's the first?" he asked, falling into her teasing mood, even as it made him remember days gone by.

"I forget," she said, then burst into laughter.

Listening to her husky voice with its intriguing little breaks, he laughed, too. She had always had the ability to make him feel better. When she was in an exuberant mood, as she was now, she was prone to laugh and tease unmercifully.

But she had also listened to his problems and shared her feelings with him...in those long ago days when they were friends.

"Coffee?" he asked, tearing himself away from the memories with an effort.

"Not on an empty stomach. Rose and I did a study, and that stuff can eat through stainless steel in three days, gospel truth." She held up a hand in a pledge of honor.

He tossed the cup into the trash bin. "How about dinner? I haven't eaten since breakfast."

"That would be great. Taylor and the babies are all asleep, so it would be a good time to go. I'll get Rose."

He nodded, but she was already gone, a whirlwind of energy, shedding radiance on all who came into her orbit.

His heart pounded suddenly. The birthing had caused some strange twists in him that afternoon. He hadn't realized it would be so emotional and affecting.

Right now, after the excitement of all that...okay, after the kiss that had seared him right down to the soles of his feet...well, he kept thinking of other things, things he hadn't let himself think of in years.

Ally stuck her head in the door. The hall light turned her blond hair into a golden halo around her slender, oval face. She had ''big'' hair. Shoulder-length, it always looked tousled. Her cheeks were always pink. As if she'd just come in from some fun exercise in the outdoors. Or climbed out of bed. His body stirred hungrily.

For a second, he considered what it would be like to share the excitement of bringing a new life into the world with a beloved mate. And the excitement of creating that new life. Heat pounded through him. There in the birthing room, as he held the two babies, an image had flashed through his mind—of him and a woman and their children....

''Ready?'' she asked.

''Yes.'' His voice was husky, sexy. He cleared his throat. ''Yes,'' he said again, more firmly this time.

Yeah, it was good that his mom would be with them.

He followed Ally along the corridor. He heard groans and pants emanating from a couple of rooms as they passed. The sounds took on a whole new meaning for him now that he knew exactly what they were. He still couldn't believe his mother had deliberately set him up for the birthing scene. He intended to ask her about that.

''Rose? We're ready,'' Ally called softly to his mom, who was still in the room with Taylor. When Rose joined them, Ally whispered, ''Let's go by the nursery.''

Spence patiently accepted the women's eagerness

to peek at the twins once more before they left. At the nursery window, he saw the babies tucked into little plastic buckets on wheels, a bright light shining down on each one. Both kids wore a tiny stocking cap on their heads and slept peacefully in spite of the lamp.

"Ohhh," Ally croaked, her voice breaking. "They are so beautiful."

A hand closed around his arm. Ally leaned against him and looked up, her eyes glowing like a laser beamed through sapphires.

"Aren't they just darling?" she crooned.

Spence squinted and tried to see what made them more beautiful than the other two babies, also under lights, in the nursery. "Well, uh, they are pretty cute."

"Hannah looks like Taylor, I think," she continued, pressing her nose to the glass. "Nicholas probably takes more after his father. What do you think?"

Spence thought women could see a lot more than men could when it came to these things. To him, they looked like...well...they looked like babies.

His mother gave a soft, feminine snort of laughter. "Don't make him perjure himself, Ally." She patted her son's other arm. "Don't worry. They'll grow on you. Let's go eat. I'm starved. How about the diner?"

They went across the street to Mom and Pop's diner. He'd grown used to seeing medical staff, still wearing their white jackets, in there, or men in suits and women in fancy dresses with stethoscopes around their necks. The diner was a hangout for all the workers from the baby clinic, hospital and professional office building across the street. The food was about ten times better than anything they could get in the medical complex.

Ally sighed as she slid into a booth. Rose sat opposite her, taking up the middle of the banquette. After a second's hesitation, Spence took the place beside his sister-in-law.

His warmth slid up her arm and down into her belly. She licked her lips. They tingled as if electricity was running lightly over them. The way it had during that impulsive kiss. She wished she hadn't done that.

She noticed Spence carefully avoided touching her. A pang of irritation shot through her as the euphoria of the births gave way to weariness. They ordered and were silent until tall frosty glasses of raspberry tea were served.

"I'm dog-tired," she stated.

"You've been working too hard," Rose admonished. "You need to watch it now that you have two babies to care for. You'll have to learn to pace yourself. Start with a good night's sleep. It will probably be your last for the next few weeks. Or years."

Ally laughed with her mom-in-law. "I've caught up on all my casework, including all the reports required by the city, county, state and federal agencies. Sometimes it seems I hardly have time for patients because of the forms I have to fill out."

As a child psychologist who scheduled in as much pro bono work as she could, Ally had to admit she had a tendency to overextend herself at times.

"But now I have a whole two weeks off," she continued. "After that, I'll be working half-time until the twins are three months old and can go to the Family Care Center."

She was aware that Spence had turned partially in the seat so that he could watch her as she talked. She suddenly felt self-conscious at his perusal. It was so odd to be…oh, nervous or something, around him, when they had once been best friends. She turned back to Rose.

"Did I tell you Taylor is going to come over to my office and help with the twins as much as she can? I'm going to insist that she let me pay her."

"I'm not sure you should encourage that," Spence spoke up, his brow furrowed into a thoughtful frown. "The courts have been very protective about returning adopted children to their birth parents the past few years."

"Taylor and I have talked about it. I want her to have a place in the children's lives. I think it's important. The situations that work best result in the birth parent becoming a big sister to the kids and the adoptive parent being the mother."

"If things work out according to plan," Spence added with a cynical inflection. "What about the father?"

She glanced at Spence. His dark brown eyes with their tiny golden flecks delved into hers. "The father…the sperm donor," she corrected, "has no place in this. He opted out when he listened to his folks and abandoned Taylor. They said she was a gold digger and had gotten pregnant to trap him into marriage. They tried to buy her off."

"Did they succeed?"

"No, she refused their money. She was working here in the diner and overheard Rose and me talking about adoption. When I came in alone, she approached me about taking her baby. It was hard for her."

Ally and Taylor had both shed tears when the nineteen-year-old had explained her plight. A lot of young women in her situation would have taken the money, had an abortion and gotten on with their lives. Ally could understand the stubborn pride that had caused Taylor to refuse the money.

Ally's folks had been middle class, but they had died when she was eleven. She had gone from being a cherished only child to an undesired duty in her aunt's life. The woman hadn't wanted to deal with the needs of a youngster or spend any money on her, either. Ally had delivered papers and worked odd jobs to earn her own spending money. Oh, yes, she understood pride very well.

Like Taylor, she had also worked her way through school, taking the courses that led to an R.N. and college degree and finishing in three years. After that, she had gone to night school while working full-time as a nurse at the hospital. With her Ph.D. in psychology, she had opened her own practice.

And she had married Jack McBride, Rose's oldest son, brother to Spence, who had been her best friend during the lonely years of living with her aunt down the road from the friendly McBride family. Sometimes she wondered if she had married Jack because she had wanted Rose for a mother.

Or maybe because of the loneliness.

Spence had made it clear they could never be anything but friends. Her college years had been divided between work and study. Lonely years. Until Jack had started to show interest in her.

Actually, he'd swept her off her feet, an action that was totally out of character for him, as she had learned during their years of marriage.

She sighed, thinking of that young girl who had wanted…had truly expected…the moon and stars and all the magic life had to offer. She wondered what had happened to that girl, then realized she knew the answer.

She'd had to grow up.

For the rest of the evening nostalgia gripped her in a vague cloud of yearning and regret. After saying goodnight to Rose and Spence, she returned to the hospital for one more peek at the twins and to chat with Taylor before visiting hours ended. Driving home, she tried to throw off the haunting emotion, but it was no use. As she turned out the light and settled into the queen-size bed, she realized she felt sorry for the girl she had once been—the one who had dared to dream.

And the birth of the twins had stirred those dreams once again.

Chapter Two

Ally threw the sheet off and sprang up as if someone had dumped a load of hot coals on the bed. She had so much to do! If everything had gone well during the night, she could bring the twins home this afternoon. She would have them to herself at last.

The qualms that coursed through her were natural. All new moms felt unsure and apprehensive about the responsibility of caring for babies. Rose would help if she needed her. She only had to call.

The sadness descended unexpectedly. In her heart, she realized, she still wanted all the things she'd once dreamed of—a husband who would share life with her, who would be there for her as she would be there for him, who would be a loving father to their children. That dream wasn't to be.

But the one about having her own family was about to come true in a big way. Twins were double trouble! Laughing, she jumped out of bed.

She dashed through her morning chores, then, taking her coffee with her, strolled through the house. She and Jack had bought the two-bedroom cottage from her aunt for the acreage that went with it.

They had planned to remodel the house before having kids. They'd wanted to put in a garden and fence off a section for a pony. Somehow the years had slipped by without their doing any of it. As Spence had mentioned, plans didn't always work out.

When she and Jack had married, she'd thought she would never be lonely again. At first, she hadn't, but somehow things had changed. Jack had become increasingly jealous of her work and her involvement with her patients after she finished her studies and set up the office.

And of his younger brother whenever Spence joined the family for holiday meals and such.

She'd had to be very careful not to mention the past adventures she and Spence had shared. She had made sure she was never alone with Spence at the family gatherings and had been careful not to tease or even talk to him very much.

Later, when she didn't conceive, Jack had become angry, as if she'd withheld a child on purpose. Their marriage had fallen upon rocky times. He had started working later and later. Last year, she'd even wondered if there was another woman. Then he had died, working alone one night, trying to finish a job by moving lumber with an old forklift.

Something had gone wrong and the stack of lumber had cascaded down on him. The doctor said he hadn't suffered. A blow to the head had killed him at once.

Small comfort in that.

She had thought, with the coming of the babies, they would have a focus in their marriage. As a psychologist, she knew how foolish it was to hope children would solve a troubled marriage, but they'd had no real problems, no crises of faith or broken vows.

Just a slow drifting apart...

Sadness trailed after her as she went into the guest bedroom. She had used it as a home office, but it would have to be the nursery until the addition on the house was completed.

Twin bassinets stood next to the wall. One was trimmed in blue, the other in yellow. They had known one baby was a boy, but hadn't been able to tell for sure about Hannah from the sonograms.

After checking the supplies of diapers, nightshirts, day outfits and bottles, which she'd done a hundred times already, she went to the door at the end of the hallway.

Two bedrooms and a bath were being added for the twins so each could have a room. The carpenter hadn't proceeded as quickly as she would have liked. The inside work remained to be done, although the outside was finished.

Baseboards were stacked in one room, paint cans

in the other. She and Rose had made curtains, which still needed to be hemmed after the rods were put up. None of that could be done until the walls and trim were finished.

She returned to the kitchen. Where was the carpenter she had hired? He was supposed to be there at seven. He liked to start early, what with the heat of summer and all, he'd told her. So where was he?

She sat at the table and debated calling his home. He got peeved if she pestered him or asked too many questions.

Men and their fragile egos.

She called the hospital and found out Taylor and the twins were doing fine. Taylor reported she was leaving the hospital with a friend soon and thanked Ally again for being with her.

After hanging up, Ally sat and stared out the window at the orchard that separated the cottage from the McBride house where Rose lived.

Spence had a neat apartment in a new building about a mile from them. She'd been there once when Rose had thrown a welcome-back dinner for him at the place.

A sigh worked its way out of her. She felt melancholy today for some reason. As if she was suffering from the postpartum depression new mothers often got.

Her thoughts drifted. She mused on her nine years of marriage and on being a widow for almost eight months. At thirty-two, she felt no wiser than she had at twenty-two, when she'd married Jack.

Or at eighteen when she'd thought friendship

would grow into love. She smiled and felt her lips tremble.

Memories. Sometimes they could weave a cloud around the heart and make a person ache for what might have been. How young she'd been at eighteen on the night of their high-school graduation....

Spence, the most popular guy in class, had broken up with a cheerleader, who was the most popular girl. The cheerleader had gone to the graduation dance with the star quarterback to get back at him. He'd dropped by Ally's house, knowing she hadn't planned on going to the dance.

She'd had few dates in high school. With delivering newspapers and baby-sitting jobs, plus working toward a nursing scholarship, she'd had very little time for extracurricular activities, and no money to buy a fancy dress.

Spence had asked her to go for a drive. She'd gone willingly. They had always been there for each other from the moment she'd come to live with her aunt. The day she arrived, he'd stopped by to see what was happening, and he'd immediately pitched in and helped carry her things inside and store them in the little sewing room that would become her bedroom for the next seven years. He'd even let her ride his new bike. They had become fast friends.

Sometimes that seemed strange to her, as if they'd been kindred souls, even as children. She'd never been as close to another person, before or since.

On that long-ago graduation night, he'd driven

out to a hiking trail that started next to the river and wound up into the mountains. To her surprise he'd had one bottle of champagne in a cooler in the back of his car. She'd laughed when she realized she was sharing a treat he'd planned for the homecoming queen, and had teased him about it.

They had talked seriously then, about the college he would attend and law school, both back east, then about her scholarship, which had come through. She'd admitted she would be glad to leave her aunt's home.

"I'm going to have my own place someday," she'd bragged.

And here she was, back in her aunt's old house. But now it was hers...hers and the twins. For the split second between one heartbeat and another, she wondered what life would have been like if Spence had been her husband, if the twins had been their babies....

When Spence had opened the bottle of champagne, he'd proposed a toast.

"To friendship. To the future. To us." She had echoed his words and raised the glass to her lips.

"Wait," he'd said. He had hooked his arm through hers. Arms linked, they had sipped the magic elixir.

It had been sweet and romantic. When the moon rose over the mountain peak and laid a sparkling trail on the swift flowing river, he had leaned over and kissed her. Full on the lips. Mouth open. Tongue gently asking for entry between her surprised lips.

Then came the rush. A wild, swift, painful re-lease of pleasure that had made her gasp.

He had deepened the kiss at that moment, taking advantage of her momentary start to delve inside and claim her mouth for his own in a way no boy had ever done. And in that instant, she had known this was a man's kiss, given to a woman. She had responded in kind.

When they had pulled apart, both had been breathing in deep, harsh drafts. They had taken an-other sip of champagne from the plastic stemmed flutes, their eyes never leaving each other as they drank a wordless toast.

When the flutes were empty, he had tossed them into the back and slid across the space between the bucket seats. Then he'd lifted her into his arms and settled her across his lap. They'd kissed again.

For her, it was as if the heavens had opened and poured all its blessings on them. Happiness, like golden raindrops, splashed through her spirit, and rainbows formed, faded and reformed behind her closed eyelids.

She'd been to parties. She'd been kissed. But not like this. Nothing would ever be like this total bliss, this blending of hearts and minds and spirits. She sensed they had changed. They had gone from best friends to lovers in a single melding of the lips and their spirits.

"You taste like honey," he murmured, leaving her mouth and tracing a path to her ear. "Like hot honey."

"Yes," she agreed. "I am hot…achy hot…"

His body pressed urgently against hers. She felt the rigid length of him against her thigh and wasn't shocked at the blatant evidence of his desire. Then she was a little shocked...at herself. She'd never been this close to a male, had never felt an erection, but the knowledge only excited her more.

Because it was Spence. And because she trusted him—her best friend, her lover. She shivered in anticipation.

"Spence," she whispered as a thread of desperation unwound inside her. "The yearning...make it go away."

"I will," he said just as fervently. "We will. Together." He caressed her back, then slipped one hand under her hair to nestle against her scalp.

This time the kiss was explosive, filled with needs they had never dared confess, much less share. She whimpered and moaned. Sometimes she sighed. The kiss went on.

Driven to boldness, she pushed her hands under his T-shirt and found the heated expanse of smooth skin laced with hard muscle. There was hair on his chest. Not a lot, but enough to fascinate while she ran her fingers through it.

He groaned and pressed her hands flat against him. "Yes, Ally, touch me. In any way you want. For as long as you want. It feels...too good," he muttered.

She thrilled at the shudder that passed through his lean, muscular body. When his hands began a gentle exploration along her waist, she held her breath, wanting...needing...

"Yes," she said on a sigh when his hand slid over her hot, hot flesh, along her back, down her sides and up her middle. He hesitated then he cupped her breast, taking its weight into his hand.

His heart pounded in unison with hers as the tension escalated to dizzy heights. Her nipple drew into a tight bud against his palm. He rubbed in circles until spirals of sensation echoed down into her core. Breaking the kiss, she pressed her face into his shoulder and bit, very gently, into the strong cords of his neck.

"I'm sorry," she murmured, appalled that she wanted to bite him. It was something she'd never done.

"No, it's okay. That didn't hurt. Bite me some more. I like it. I like anything you do."

His smile flashed white and quick in the deepening night. Her smile was hesitant. She'd never felt this way, so certain and yet so unsure. It was odd...

He dipped his head and nibbled at her lips. She caught his bottom lip between her teeth and sucked. He drew a harsh breath. Against her breasts, his heart bucked like a rodeo bronco gone wild. Hers went wild with him.

"Ally, I want to see you. Do you mind?"

The question was undemanding, eager but patient. Tears sprang into her eyes. "You are so gentle," she said.

"I want to be gentle. I wouldn't do anything to scare you. Do you believe me?"

"Yes."

He urged her to rest against the car door. His hands went to her blouse. One by one, he unfastened the row of tiny buttons shaped like bows, white against the blue cotton. Her white bra looked dainty, almost flimsy against her tan. She moved instinctively to cross her hands over her chest, then placed them instead around him, sliding one behind him, the other resting on his upper arm.

He smiled again, his gaze catching hers and holding it while he laid a broad hand over her tummy and caressed. "You are so innocent," he said, almost as if he spoke to himself.

"I am...I mean, I haven't..."

"I know what you mean. Neither have I."

He dropped a quick kiss on her mouth, then, looking into her eyes, slid his hands behind her. She felt him pause, then his fingers glided beneath her bra on each side of the hook that held it closed.

"Are you comfortable with this? I can stop at any time. Just say the word."

She considered, then shook her head, not wanting him to stop. He understood her meaning.

After unfastening the hooks he pushed the blouse off her shoulders. The bra came with it. He carefully laid them over the steering wheel. His eyes came back to her.

"I'm not—"

"Shh," he said. "You're beautiful. May I?"

Spellbound, she watched as he tested each tip with his tongue. She closed her eyes and rubbed his shoulders, his neck, threaded her fingers into his hair. He kissed her breasts until they tingled. He

drew magic circles that spun off madly into her body and collided with the spirals he'd already caused.

"I want us to touch…my skin, yours," she tried to explain. "I need to touch all over.…"

He leaned away from the seat and stripped his T-shirt off over his head. When he pulled her against him, hot smooth flesh against hot smooth flesh, she trembled as their need reached the flaming point.

"Spence, that's…that's…it feels…"

"Incredible," he murmured. "Ah, Ally, you are so incredibly sweet."

She writhed against him. He caressed her with sweet movements and shrugs of his body against hers, satisfying and feeding her passion at the same instant.

He fed on her lips. She sipped from his. She learned the shape of his teeth, the points and edges, that the bottom one wasn't quite even with the others. He explored the texture of her mouth, the smooth flesh behind her lips, showed her the velvety tracing of tongue on tongue.

His movements were sure. There was a maturity about him, a manliness, she had never noticed. It reached deep into her soul.

In turn, she felt a blossoming inside, in a hidden glen that now felt the kiss of the sun warming the loamy earth, readying it for spring and new growth.

"Straddle me," he requested.

His hands on her waist lifted her. He had strength she hadn't suspected, her weight easy to him. She

swung her leg over his thighs. He settled her against him.

"Oh," she said as entirely new sensations erupted.

"Now be still," he ordered and gave a short, self-deprecating laugh. "You have me on the edge. One slip and I'll go right over."

His confession thrilled her in ways she couldn't name. Her blood flowed with golden lava, with champagne bubbles and laughter.

"Me, too," she said, biting desperately, carefully, on his shoulder. "I'm the same, so...so..." She didn't know the words.

"Very much so," he agreed.

He found the bow that closed the drawstring to her summer slacks. It opened when he tugged. Then he slipped his hands inside the material and cupped her bottom. She fit her breasts to his chest.

"We're hot, you and I," she whispered. "Our skin, it's like fire on fire."

"I went up in smoke a long time ago. You're just now catching up."

When he moved slightly, she gasped as tremor after tremor of need arced through her.

"See?" he said.

He smiled again, and it was so tender she could have wept had there been time. But he was kissing her again, and the stars dropped from their orbits and into her soul.

She didn't know how long they kissed and touched each other. Forever, it seemed.

The moon spread a molten path of silver across the river as it rose higher. Still they kissed.

And kissed.

At last she knew it had to stop or they had to go further. "This isn't enough," she complained, panting lightly, placing carefully spaced kisses along his collarbone and down his chest as far as she could reach. "This has got to...to finish."

He groaned and caught her to him, pulling her hands behind her back and holding them there.

"Let me touch you," she requested and pressed hard against the ridge in his jeans.

"No."

She rose slightly on her knees and rubbed against him.

"Don't."

This time the tone was stern, older, the disciplined male taking command instead of letting her do as she wished in their love play.

"Why?"

He kissed her eyes instead of answering when she stared at him in the shadowy moonlight. She leaned farther back and looked at him, beginning to feel hurt and confused.

"Don't hate me," he said.

She was surprised. "I don't. I never would—"

He laid his mouth over hers until the words were stilled. "We have something special. We shouldn't have... It was my fault. I shouldn't have let it go this far. I didn't mean to—"

"What did you mean to do?"

"Talk." He smiled briefly, almost sadly. "Share

a kiss for old times' sake. Not this…not this far, not this much. It was a…surprise.''

His explanation made no sense. ''What?'' she asked. ''What was a surprise?''

He lifted her from him and moved to his seat. She suddenly felt chilled. When he handed her the clothing, she pulled it on hurriedly. After yanking his T-shirt over his head, he turned back to her, lifting her face to his with a finger under her chin. His expression was gentle, kind.

''Don't be ashamed,'' he ordered, reading her reaction correctly. ''This was natural. It just wasn't what I had planned. You're my friend. I want to keep it that way.''

Pride made her face him without flinching. ''I understand. I'd better get home. I have to get up at five to pick up my papers.'' Fatigue swept over her as reality shoved its way into her consciousness.

He had driven them to town, away from the moonlight and its induced madness, her heart too numb to ache. Yet…

Ally picked up her coffee cup. It was empty. She realized she'd been sitting there for an hour, reliving the past. Frowning, she jumped to her feet. The day was wasting. Where were the men who were supposed to be working on the house?

The ringing of the doorbell jarred Ally out of a sound sleep. She sat up on the sofa and wondered who was so darned impatient at her front door. She noted the afternoon was half over and still no carpenters.

She checked the peephole and opened the door. "Hello, James. What happened to you?"

The carpenter's son stood on the porch, his arm in a cast from fingers to elbow. "Uh, Dad and I, we had a wreck this morning on our way over."

"Oh, no! How's your father? Is he hurt?"

James nodded, his summer-blond hair falling over his forehead in a carefree manner, belying the seriousness of his face. "He's in the hospital, leg broke in three places. They'll have to put pins in it."

"I'm so sorry. Was anyone else in the truck? Your mom?"

"No, just the two of us. The guy in the dump truck wasn't hurt at all. He just barged through a red light and mowed us down."

She *tsked* in sympathy. "Come in out of the heat," she invited, opening the door wider. "I have some tea—"

"I need to get back to the hospital and stay with my mom. They're gonna operate on the old man as soon as the surgeon gets there. He's out playing golf or something." He gestured vaguely with one hand. "I don't think we'll get back to your job for two or three months."

She thought that was an optimistic estimate. "Don't worry about it. I can do the painting myself."

He nodded, looking miserable. "I called several buddies but they're all working on the new construction job over on the other side of town. You

know, the fancy apartment complex they put in over by the lake.''

She knew where he meant. Spence had moved into a bachelor apartment there last February. The planned community was modern and had lots of activities for singles, she'd heard.

''Don't worry about a thing here,'' she assured the young carpenter. ''I'll take care of it. Or it'll be waiting for you when you're able to work again.''

''Thanks. Well, I'd better run.''

''Tell your dad I said hello and to take care. You, too.''

He nodded and loped off, his hair flopping against his collar until he pulled on a baseball cap, the bill backwards. She smiled, feeling much older than the injured twenty-five-year-old. Seven years. It could be the difference between one lifetime and the next.

Of course, one night could do the same.

After those wild kisses, from the time Spence had dropped her off, making sure she was safely inside her aunt's house, and the dawn of the next day, she had aged considerably. The bubbles had evaporated from her blood and her mind. She had taken a good hard look at herself.

Her looks were not extraordinary. Her thick hair, which had some natural curl, was okay, she supposed. And when she was eighteen, it still had some gold in it. Her friends at school had been envious. Big blond hair was in.

Her eyes were a nice shade of blue, but her lashes were short and a medium sort of brown. So were

her eyebrows. Her hair would probably be the same when she grew older.

But she didn't mind working hard. And she was well-organized. She could take on a lot of tasks, even drudgery.

With her aunt's blessings and some savings left over from her parents' insurance, plus her paper route, baby-sitting and lawn mowing money, she'd started classes at the local college the week after graduation and had devoted the next six years of her life to earning degrees, with only a short break for a honeymoon between classes.

Going into the bedroom to change into fresh clothes before picking up the twins, she wondered when she'd had time to date Jack, not to mention get married and take over home responsibilities, too. She must have been crazy.....

No. Lonely. The haunting sadness strummed through her again. Her college days had been busy, but she lived them basically alone, running from work to class and back to work. There'd been little time for fun.

During her senior year, her aunt had decided to sell the house, the only home Ally had known since she was eleven, and move to a retirement community in a warmer climate.

When her aunt had told her, Ally had realized she would have no one nearby. She'd lived in an apartment in Durango while completing her studies, but she'd spent one Sunday each month with her only relative.

At least it had been contact with a person who

had some kind of bond with her. In fact, she and her aunt had dealt very well with each other once she was grown.

Ally thought the responsibility for rearing a child had weighed on her aunt, who had never been around children much. Now they visited once or twice a year, usually with Ally going down to the senior citizens' community at Tucson in early spring and her aunt coming to Buttonwood for Thanksgiving. It was a satisfying arrangement.

She wondered if the visits would continue now that she had two children to raise. That would probably frighten her aunt into moving to Florida or somewhere equally remote.

Grabbing her handbag, she headed for the garage, her spirits high once more as she went to claim the children she'd wanted for so long. She laughed as she backed out of the drive, the two infant seats already strapped into the back of the family-size vehicle.

One thing for sure, she wouldn't be lonely for the next eighteen to twenty years.

Chapter Three

Ally discovered Rose wasn't at the clinic when she stopped by the administrative office after signing the insurance forms and paying the hospital bills. The older woman had gone home with a migraine.

A tremor of unease ran over her. Her mom-in-law was supposed to help her with the twins that evening, in case she had trouble getting them settled.

She could manage. After all, babies slept most of the time. She had a fresh supply of formula in neat little plastic pouches, the twin bassinets were ready and boxes of diapers and infant gowns were stored in the closet.

"Is Taylor still here?" she asked Rose's secretary.

"She's checked out. She said to tell you she had a paper to turn in tomorrow, but would be in touch."

Ally nodded and smiled as if she didn't have a qualm in the world about taking home two babies and being responsible for them for the next eighteen years…all by herself.

She suddenly felt young and vulnerable, the way she had at eleven when she'd arrived in Buttonwood, with only her clothes and a favorite doll, to live with her aunt. Or when she went off to college, living in one room in an old Victorian house and working two jobs to make her own way.

This was a far cry from those days, she reminded herself. She was an adult and a child psychologist. She knew all about children. *Sure, from a textbook standpoint,* a less confident part of her replied.

Yes, well…

She hurried down the corridor to the nursery. Rachel Arquette was on duty. The nurse was pretty, young, single…and pregnant. She wasn't saying a word about the father. Although Ally had heard the gossip going around, she didn't believe for an instant it could be Dennis Reid, who was chief of staff at the clinic. He was old enough to be Rachel's father, for Pete's sake.

"Rachel, hi," Ally said upon reaching the desk. "How are the twins?"

Rachel put away the folder she'd been reading. Although she smiled, her eyes had a certain harried look. Ally had always felt a kinship with the quiet nurse…maybe as one lost soul to another?

She pushed the thought aside as another nurse bustled out of the nursery. Ally smiled in relief at seeing Nell Hastings on duty.

Nell had taken care of the twins at the birthing. She was a delight to work with—calm in an emergency, soothing and kind in her dealings with nervous mothers and fathers, and simply wonderful with newborns.

"Well, here's our mom," Nell said cheerfully. "Hope you had a good night's sleep."

Her eyes twinkled with humor. Nell was such a contrast to her older sister, Blanche, who was one of the town's two main gossips.

"Are the twins ready to go?" Ally asked with more poise than she felt.

"Yep, fed, burped and changed. The little angels are sleeping. Finally," Nell added with a chuckle.

Ally's heart lurched. "Did they have a restless night?"

"A tad," Rachel spoke up. "They'll be okay."

"I'll help you out to the car," Nell volunteered. "Are you parked at the front?"

"Yes. I signed all the papers before coming up."

"The office called up clearance." Nell bustled off. "Let's get the babies. You have any questions?"

"Not that I can think of."

Ally took one baby, her hands shaking just a tiny bit, while Nell carried the other. At the car, the nurse strapped them into the infant seats with the skill of long practice. The darlings slept right through the process.

"Well, thanks," Ally said.

Nell patted her back. "Sleep when they do, if you can. Tuck them against you if they get to crying. They're used to sleeping in cramped quarters." Her smile was reassuring.

"Right."

Ally drove off at five miles per hour, suddenly afraid that someone was going to hit her car and injure the twins, afraid she wouldn't see them in time, afraid she wouldn't notice a red light and would run through it....

Her knuckles were white all the way to the cottage. She parked at home with a sigh of relief, as if she'd completed a major and dangerous feat.

Unbuckling Nicholas, she carried him into the house and gently tucked him into a bassinet, then returned for Hannah. Both slept peacefully throughout the transition. Ally checked that the baby monitor was on, then tiptoed out of the nursery and into the kitchen.

Well, there was nothing to this, she decided four hours later, checking the sleeping twins for the umpteenth time. She'd been worried for nothing. She could relax.

She nearly jumped out of her skin when the doorbell rang. She closed the nursery door and dashed lightly into the living room. Her eyes widened when she recognized Spence outside the door.

"Hi," she said, opening up and letting him in. "What are you doing in this neighborhood?"

Stupid question. His mother lived a quarter mile up the road. He was on his way there, most likely.

He was dressed in blue shorts and a polo shirt. She noticed that his arms and legs were very tan. She imagined him playing golf or tennis with all the attractive single women at the apartment complex.

"Providing dinner," he explained. "I didn't know if you would remember to eat, this being your first night with the twins. I brought over sandwiches—beef tongue, sliced eggs, kosher dills and hot mustard with a touch of garlic."

Ally hid a smile. Spence prided himself on his gourmet touch with sandwiches. His friends thought his combinations were weird. Spence cheerfully ignored their comments.

"Oh, thanks. That was thoughtful of you. The twins are sleeping, so everything is fine."

"Great. Got a cold beer? It's a furnace out today."

Ally stared after him while he walked in, closed the door and kicked off his sneakers. He headed for the kitchen. She followed, her mind in a whirl.

"I don't have any beer. Have you been playing tennis?" she asked, placing the bag of food on the table.

Another stupid question. It was none of her business.

"No, helping Johnny put in a drip system over at his place. Claire wants to do a native plant garden. Your aunt knew a lot about that stuff. I told Claire you could give her some advice on what to plant."

He helped himself to a can of soda and rubbed

the icy container over his forehead before popping it open and taking a long drink.

"Well, I know a little," she admitted. "My aunt let me help her pick out plants. How are Claire and Johnny doing with their new baby? Lucy—isn't that her name?"

"Yes. They're doing okay. Johnny says she's sleeping all night now. You want a root beer?"

When she nodded, he plucked one from the fridge, nudged the door shut with his hip and settled at the table.

"I'm starved," he continued. "Don't bother with a plate for me. I won't need one." He dug in.

Ally put two paper plates on the table anyway and took a seat across from him. She felt funny with him there. It was the first time they'd been alone since…since…high-school graduation night.

Heat rushed to her face for no reason. That ill-advised episode was behind them. She would be wise to forget it had ever happened, just as he had.

She took a sip of root beer, then unwrapped the other sandwich, touched again by his thoughtfulness. The inexplicable tenderness she'd experienced toward him at the hospital returned.

From the baby monitor, she heard soft noises, as if one of the twins was restless. She tensed, but neither cried. They were certainly sleeping a long time.

She wanted to comment on this, but Spence had made it clear with his brief responses to her questions about the other couple that he wasn't inter-

ested in discussing babies and such. The silence stretched between them. He didn't seem to notice.

Irritation pricked at her. She knew it was perfectly irrational, but his hearty appetite and indifference to conversation made her angry. She was jumpy with the sleeping children in the house. It would have been nice to discuss this natural state caused by being a new parent. Once, she wouldn't have hesitated to pour her heart out to him.

But not now.

After eating the meal, she tossed her used plate in the trash and sipped the root beer. Spence polished off his food in short order.

"Ahh," he murmured. "I might make it through the night. Got any dessert?"

"There's sherbet in the freezer, cookies in the pantry." She frowned as he rummaged through her shelves.

"Nonfat," he said, reading the label on the cookies with a grimace. "What's wrong with good old-fashioned butter? Has everyone gone mad?"

He was teasing. She knew that. It didn't make her feel any better. "Some of us have to watch our weight," she informed him rather tartly, although she forced herself to put a smile behind the words.

He swung around and looked her over from head to foot. "Do you watch yours?"

"Yes."

The heat poured over her again as his eyes continued to study her. Once she would have told him all her worries. Not that she had any great ones, she

quickly assured herself. She was just jumpy because of the twins.

"Do you think the twins are sleeping a long time?" she asked, then wished she hadn't.

"How long have they been asleep?"

"Since I brought them home from the hospital." She glanced at the clock. "Four hours."

"Hmm, that doesn't sound long."

"Babies usually eat every three or four hours." She stared at the monitor, then the clock again.

Spence narrowed his eyes and observed her for a long minute. "Well, let's go look at them."

She stood when he did. He motioned for her to lead the way. They walked down the short hall. Since he was in his socks, he made no sound at all. She tried to walk as softly.

After easing the door open, she tiptoed across the nursery and surveyed the sleeping babies. Her heart melted. They looked like cherubs, sweet and innocent and trusting. She smiled at Spence and pointed toward the door. They quietly left. He closed the door behind them.

"What are you thinking?" Spence asked, a curious note in his baritone voice as they returned to the kitchen.

"How innocent they are. How trusting." She shook her head. "I don't feel worthy of it."

"Mom said you would make the perfect mother."

Ally glanced up at him in surprise. "You discussed me and the children with Rose?"

"Of course." His eyes locked with hers. "She

worried about you during the winter. After Jack was gone. She said your grief was very deep and very lonely."

Ally looked away from his probing gaze, feeling the strange loneliness descend on her again. She didn't understand it at all.

"He was at work. Alone. We had both worked late that day. I didn't think to check on him when I got in and he wasn't home."

She stopped, wondering if she'd given too much away about the last months and years of her marriage. She would never discuss her relationship with Jack with anyone, especially Spence. Although he had never said anything, she had always sensed his disapproval of the marriage.

"Let it go," Spence advised. "It was an accident, one of those things that happen and you can't do a damned thing about it because it's too late."

The harshness of his voice startled her. She wondered what had happened in his personal life to make him speak in that tone of unrelenting certainty and bitter regret.

Sympathy stirred in her. She had imagined him swinging lightly from girl to girl, the way he had in high school, and never settling on one for long. Maybe he had been hurt in the past. If so, he hadn't shared it with her or Rose or Jack, not that she knew of.

Not that he would share anything with Jack. The two brothers had represented the epitome of sibling rivalry and the very opposites in personalities.

Where Jack had been introspective and intent, a

man who took responsibility seriously, Spence had been carefree and laughing. Not that Spence was irresponsible. Far from it. He just had a more tolerant view of the world. He had made life bearable during the difficult time when she had come to live with her aunt. He had shared his family with her—

She shied away from the past and its memories. There was the future to think about. She had the sole responsibility for those two darling twins. Life would be far from lonely from now on.

Giving Spence a radiant smile, she said, "I'm sure Nicholas and Hannah will keep me far too busy to dwell on the past and its mistakes, whatever they were."

"Such as your marriage?" he asked in a deadly quiet manner, his eyes fastening on her again.

For a second she couldn't move or think. He *had* thought the marriage was a mistake. Hurt flooded through her, exposing pain she hadn't realized she felt. Maybe an orphan hadn't been a good enough match—

No, Spence wouldn't think such a thing. It was something else, but she didn't know what. As she stared at him, perplexed by the hidden nuances of his words and expression, his face softened.

"It's okay. It wasn't your fault."

She didn't know what he was talking about. "What?"

"Nothing." His face assumed its usual devil-may-care grin, effectively hiding the inner thoughts he guarded.

At that moment, a soft snuffle came over the

monitor. It was followed by a wail. A second cry chimed in.

She and Spence laughed at the same time.

"Looks like you're going to be busy. Duty calls, Mom," he teased. "Need a hand with the feeding?"

"Yes." She led the way to the nursery, wishing she hadn't sounded so grateful.

"Okay, how do you do this?" he asked cheerfully, watching as she scooped Hannah into her arms.

He mimicked her gestures. Returning to the kitchen, she heated the formula pouches in warm water just enough to take the chill off. The twins wailed the whole time.

"Okay, Uncle Spence, let's see how well that famous charm works in this situation," she challenged, handing him one of the pouches.

He gave her a sidelong glance. "The McBride charm never fails. Remember that."

She didn't have to. She had never forgotten, she realized as they settled into the chairs. The babies stopped crying and nursed hungrily.

"Hah, that's how you stop the screaming," Spence stated in satisfaction. "You plug up the holes."

Watching him with Nicholas, that funny feeling came back. This time it reached all the way to the core of her being. Be careful, she warned herself without defining exactly what the danger was.

Thirty minutes later, they put the twins back to

bed—fed, burped and diapers changed. Spence handled that part with aplomb, too.

"How did you know to come over?" she thought to ask when they settled in the living room to catch the news on television. "You didn't just happen by with two of your famous gourmet sandwiches."

"Mom called and said she had a migraine and asked me to give you a hand. She said you'd be nervous with new babies in the house."

"I was." She sighed and rubbed the muscles in her neck. "I'm supposed to know all about children and their behavior, but it seems different, harder, when the kids are your own. Not that I had them. I mean—"

"I understand." His gaze was kind.

She realized she had never wanted kindness from him, not by itself. It hadn't been enough. What would have been? She couldn't think of an answer to that.

"The problem with both kids and court cases is that they don't follow the textbook examples, do they?"

"Not at all," she said, grateful for his lighter tone.

He left when the twins were settled again. She stood at the door and watched him head out of the driveway. He waved before turning onto the county road and driving off.

She felt oddly bereft as she wandered through the empty house. No, not empty. She went to look at the babies.

They were sleeping peacefully. As she watched them, her heart filled with so much love she ached. Hers. Hers alone.

She sighed shakily and went to prepare for bed. She'd better sleep in case they woke early.

The wails reached through the veil of sleep and brought Ally straight up. She pushed the hair off her face and stared at the clock.

Five twenty-four. The sun was barely up.

She rushed into the nursery, but too late. Nicholas's cries had roused Hannah, and now she wailed, too.

"There, there," Ally crooned.

Not that it did any good. The twins continued their duet. She didn't know what was wrong. She'd been up less than an hour ago and fed and changed them. Also an hour before that. And another one before that.

In fact, she hadn't slept more than an hour in any one time period for the past three nights.

Sleep when they did?

Ha! She had barely gotten a moment to shower and change clothes before the familiar cries started up again.

"Now look," she said upon entering the nursery, "you're going to have to be more specific. Tell Mommy what's wrong."

It had seemed a bit strange the first day, referring to herself as "Mommy," but now she felt more comfortable with it. In fact, she felt well broken into the role.

She smiled and yawned, then laid a soothing hand on each plump tummy and patted gently. Nick fell asleep. Hannah stared at her, her baby-blue eyes wide and round as if sizing her up.

Ally bent over the bassinet. "Hi, big girl," she whispered. "The sun is up. You can go to sleep now."

Which is exactly what the twins had been doing—crying all night, then sleeping during the day.

After another moment, Hannah's eyes blinked a couple of times, then closed and stayed that way.

Ally tiptoed out. She put on the coffee, washed up and dressed, then sat in the sunny kitchen and read the paper after eating her usual bowl of cereal with a banana.

Restless, she dusted and mopped the small house, then went into the new rooms. Hmm, she had brushes and rollers. There was nothing much to painting. The kids would sleep all morning, and she had nothing better to do....

Spence hung up the phone and sat staring into the middle distance for a half minute afterward. Another strange call from his mom. She had a headache and Ally needed help and could he run over to see what was wrong?

Worry sliced through him. It wasn't like Ally to ask for help and his mom had never had headaches in the past that he could recall. He would talk to Ally. Maybe together they could talk Rose into having a thorough physical. He glanced down at his clothes.

His jeans were ragged but clean. Same for the old but comfortable work shirt he'd thrown on after his shower. He slipped his bare feet into the loafers he wore on the boat. He'd spent the day overhauling the engine.

As he drove over to Ally's cottage, a new worry added to his concern. He was much too eager to see her.

He had missed his best friend, he realized. She had been his confidante from their first meeting when they'd both been eleven. Not even his partner, whom he admired tremendously, could fill the void of that lost friendship.

Every light in the house was on when he turned into the driveway. His heartbeat sped up. He imagined her hurt...ill.... Nah, if it were serious, his mom would have said so.

He rang the doorbell, feeling somewhat foolish. What should he say—"Hi, I heard you needed help and thought I'd drop in at ten-thirty at night"?

Hardly. He could say he was driving by and saw the lights on. He'd decided to stop and see how things were going. That sounded plausible.

When a moment had passed without answer, he pressed the doorbell again, more insistently this time. When the door opened, the words he had prepared disappeared from his mind.

"What's happened?" he asked, somewhat stunned by her appearance.

He had never seen Ally look so unlike her usual composed, efficient self. Her hair was pulled back in a ponytail, sort of. Clumps had come loose and

hung down her neck. A strand was draped over her face. She flicked it back impatiently.

"What are you doing here?" she asked, obviously not beside herself with joy at seeing him.

"I was driving by," he began and saw skepticism flash into her eyes. "Mom called and said you needed help."

To his shock, tears sprang into her eyes.

"I don't."

Her voice wavered. He frowned as she stopped and visibly tried to compose herself. He stepped forward, forcing her to move back, and closed the door, cutting off the hot July air streaming into the air-conditioned house.

"What's that noise?" he demanded.

"Nick and Hannah. They're crying."

"Oh." He glanced at the monitor on the table. The sound was low, but both children were wailing. "Hadn't you better see about them?"

She swallowed as if holding back grief. "I have. They've been fed and burped and diapered and rocked and sung to and walked with...."

Again her voice wobbled and broke. She pressed her lips together. He stared at the tears that gathered, thicker and thicker, on her lower lashes, but refused to fall.

"They don't like me," she said with an air of abject misery. "I've tried. I've done everything the books suggested. They don't like it here."

He started to smile at this overly dramatic statement, but stopped when one tear then another slipped down her haggard face. Ally the competent,

the independent, was frazzled. He had the strongest urge to reach out and take her into his arms. Just to comfort her, of course.

"Let's see what we can do," he suggested, gesturing toward the nursery. "Misery loves company, I've heard. I can walk one while you walk the other."

She wiped her hands across her eyes the way a tired four-year-old might do, gave him a wan smile and led the way down the short hall. The noise was jarring when she opened the door.

"Hey, there, fella," Spence said in a hearty tone, scooping up the first baby.

"That's Hannah," Ally corrected. "I'll take her. You take Nick. He doesn't want me to touch him."

Spence wanted to say something to reassure her, but nothing came to mind. He didn't have the foggiest idea what babies liked or didn't like. He did know that *he* didn't like Ally to be so stressed out. She looked weary and ready to cave in. That wasn't the image he had of her.

For a second another picture planted itself firmly in his mind—Ally in his arms, giddy with champagne and graduation and his kisses....

His body flushed with desire. He turned so his back was to Ally. She didn't need to see the evidence of his reaction to that memory. She hadn't wanted him. She'd married his brother, who had never appreciated her sunny nature, her drive and compassion and trustworthiness.

They exchanged babies.

"There, there," he said, jostling Nick up and

down while Ally paced the room and made similar noises.

Nick shut up and stared up at him with keen, unblinking eyes. The kid knew more than he let on, Spence decided. That gaze was too candid, too wise, not to see the truth.

What truth?

That he had coveted his brother's wife? That he hadn't dared to stay around them or he might have knocked Jack's teeth down his throat for being impatient with Ally's compassion for a stray animal, her concern for children, her sense of the ridiculous when she was in a happy, teasing mood?

He hadn't seen any of that in her in years. He missed it as much as he did their long talks about beauty and truth and all the great ideas of life.

"See?" she demanded. "Nick likes you."

"When was the last time you slept?" Spence asked, seeing past her querulous accusation to the exhaustion in her eyes.

"When was the last time you were here?"

"The day you brought the twins home. Wednesday."

"That was it."

She bounced Hannah the way he was doing Nick. The sobs died off to an occasional sniffle.

"Three days since you had a night's sleep? No wonder you're tired. Listen, Johnny said kids often need time to adjust to a new place, new people. Think of the trauma these two went through, leaving a nice warm comfy place for the cruel harsh world. Anybody would cry over that."

That brought a faint smile.

He looked more closely at her. "You have little white speckles in your hair and on your face."

She nodded. "I painted one of the new bedrooms today. Most of it. Until they started crying around four this afternoon. Nick hates me. Except when he eats, he cries even when I carry him around."

"Why the hell...heck were you painting? You can hire somebody to do stuff like that."

"The carpenter had a wreck. His leg is broken. His son, who was supposed to do painting, has a broken wrist. They won't be able to finish for months. I couldn't find anyone else. I called everywhere."

"So you had to do it yourself." He scowled at her. "That is so typical. Ally, the wonder girl, won't ask for help. You wouldn't let me deliver your papers that time the dog bit you and made you fall off your bike."

"It was my job. And your bike. You loaned it to me so I could finish faster."

"I *gave* it to you. It was my old one, but no, you had to pay me for it. You were always stubborn."

Her chin jutted out. He remembered that look very well, the one that said she wasn't taking anything from anyone, including what she deemed charity.

Glaring at her, he felt something happen inside him, something odd and unnerving, like an earthquake in the very core of his being. In its aftermath, a part of him suddenly ached and he didn't know

which part it was. But he was pretty sure he knew what caused the sudden tumult.

Ally.

The situation with her was worrisome. She looked young and defenseless and too proud by half. He wanted to help her as he had tried to do in the past. He wanted her to accept his help, her pride be damned.

He wanted to kiss her senseless.

The admission startled him. It shook him right down to the conscience that had plagued him when he'd been tempted to get one up on Jack during their competitive youth. He had played fair, he reminded that inner voice. He'd stayed away from Ally that summer, when she and Jack had gotten engaged. He'd treated her as a sister during the years of their marriage. He'd been fair....

Nick started crying. Hannah chimed in. Spence looked at Ally. Tears were running down her face, too.

The tension grew inside him. Along with it came the hunger. He wanted to make love to her until she no longer looked so woebegone. He wanted her happy and joyous, her eyes shining the way they had that night when they'd parked in the moonlight and talked and kissed until they were both breathless and flushed with need.

He groaned. Maybe he shouldn't have moved back to Buttonwood.

Chapter Four

The night grew long as the twins alternated between wakefulness and restless periods of sleep. As usual, they slept no more than an hour or so at a time.

"You don't have to stay," Ally told Spence shortly before two a.m. "There's no need for both of us to lose sleep." She managed a smile even though she dreaded the idea of being alone again.

Spence was right—misery did love company. It was reassuring to have his calm presence at hand, softly scolding Nick for being such a pain, reminding the baby in a serious tone that real men don't carry on like this, and telling Hannah no one liked wailing women.

"I slept last night," Spence said cheerfully.

"You get some shut-eye. I'll take care of these two."

"No, I meant—"

"I know what you meant." With hands on her shoulders, he gave her a little push toward her bedroom. "Go on."

She shook her head. It didn't feel right. The children were her responsibility, not his. She stifled a yawn. "I'll rest on the sofa for a bit," she decided. "They'll be awake again soon."

"Okay."

His smile appeared innocent enough, but his eyes held a twinkle she hadn't seen in years. It meant he was up to some mischief, usually at her expense.

She spent all of five seconds trying to figure out what devious plan he might have in mind, then gave it up. She settled in the corner of the sofa, tucked her feet close to her and closed her eyes...just for a moment.

The kids were asleep once more. Spence, after walking both babies for an hour so Ally could sleep, returned to the living room. He settled in the easy chair. It was made for a woman's shoulders, not a man's. He twisted uncomfortably a couple of times, then moved to the other end of the sofa.

He kicked off his shoes and propped his feet on the coffee table. He'd seen Ally do this, so he knew it was okay in her house. That was one thing he liked about her—she believed in comfort first.

He'd tried living with a woman for a short time after getting out of law school and setting up his

practice in Durango. She'd driven him crazy with her finicky ways. He hadn't been allowed—*allowed*, for Pete's sake—to put his feet on his own furniture.

Ally had never been like that. From his observations, she'd been easy to live with. But Jack...

Jack had been impatient when she worked long hours and dinner was late, but she had never told him to fix his own meal, not that Spence knew of. Some men didn't appreciate what a gold mine they had in their wives.

Spence realized his thoughts were straying into forbidden territory. Jack and Ally's marriage had been nobody's business but their own. He shut down the past and directed his mind to the law cases he was handling.

He'd filed the appeal for the rancher on the mineral-rights lease. Now he needed some evidence that the mining company hadn't upheld its end of their mining contracts with other landowners and had, in fact, polluted the land instead of digging filter ponds and using other conservation techniques as agreed on in the contracts.

Slumping deeper into the comfortable sofa, he yawned and wondered how long before his niece and nephew woke again. He felt a soft touch on his hip. Looking down, he saw a narrow, dainty foot resting against him.

Ally sighed and shifted so that her head lay on the sofa arm. She stretched out farther so that both feet were planted firmly against him. Her toes were cold.

He pulled the afghan off the sofa back and tossed it over her, then rested his arm across her legs. Another yawn caught up with him. Drowsily he thought of another night, one when they'd been younger, innocent, ignorant of life…and of sex. Her lips had been so sweet.

For a while, he let his mind wander down a path he'd thought of often in the year after her marriage to his brother. What if, instead of being noble and honorable and all that, he had made love to Ally that long-ago graduation night? What if she'd gotten pregnant?

He would have married her, of course. At once. No question about that. The twins might have been his—

No. Ally was barren.

He'd assumed the couple hadn't had time for children, but Jack had once indicated Ally wanted them very much. His brother had seemed to resent that fact. Spence, thinking the problem was Jack, had tried to tactfully offer to be a sperm donor. Jack had nearly socked him. He had also informed Spence the problem wasn't with *him.*

So it must have been with Ally. The adoption confirmed that fact.

Spence observed her, his eyes half-closed as the need for sleep pushed wakefulness and control further from his conscious mind. Her hair spread out in lustrous tangles over the dark blue plaid material of the sofa. He remembered how it had felt in his hands—soft and silky, as thick as a collie's pelt when he ran his fingers through it.

And her skin. As soft as Hannah's.

He'd touched her back, along her sides, then finally her breasts. They had been small and firm. Her nipples had beaded against his fingers. It had driven him wild....

Desire surged in him now, a hot liquid need that beat through his blood like lava, melting everything that stood in its way. Such as the fact that she was his sister-in-law, and she had chosen his brother over him?

Grow up, he told himself, but not very forcefully. He wasn't a kid anymore, fighting with Jack over who got the biggest piece of pie, the first shot with the new basketball or any of the thousand other things they used to compete over. Ally hadn't been one of those things.

He yawned again and rubbed a hand over his face. He should stay awake so he could go to the twins as soon as they cried. Ally needed her rest.

Her toes moved against his thigh. He slipped a hand under the afghan and covered them. Cold feet, warm heart. That was Ally.

A smile tugged at the corners of his mouth. On graduation night, she'd been more than warm. She'd been hot, the same as he'd been. Hot, responsive, hungry...

He'd never wanted a woman as much, not before, not since. They would have been the first for each other. He wished he hadn't stopped. He wished he'd made love to her.

But she'd been his best friend, and they'd both

had college to get through, then graduate school. The time hadn't been right for either of them.

Not then, not later, not ever.

His body ached as need surged anew. He resolutely pushed the past behind the closed door of his youth and the things that could never be. Being here like this, helping her with her babies, that was what had brought the old memories to the surface. He hadn't thought of graduation night in years…not in years.

A whimper caught his attention. He eased up from the sofa and went quickly to the nursery before the baby could erupt into full voice and wake the other twin.

Too late, he realized as another whimper joined the first soft snuffles. He closed the door behind him.

"Okay, gang, here's what we're going to do," he told the two wide-eyed babies. "We're going to be quiet so your mommy can sleep."

He smiled as he called Ally by the name. It seemed odd and yet so right.

Hannah quieted down and stared at him with her big, baby-blue eyes. Nick opened up for a loud wail.

Spence lifted the six-pound boy and juggled him up and down. No use. Nick let out another cry, then screwed up his face as if preparing to go at it for a while. Spence, desperate, acted without thinking. He stuck his finger into the kid's mouth.

Nick looked surprised, then settled to some serious sucking on Spence's little finger.

"Well, fella, if that satisfies you, who am I to complain?" Spence inquired.

After checking on Hannah, who was trying to get all ten fingers in her mouth, he went to the kitchen with Nick, heated up the container of formula and returned to the bedroom. Nick downed nearly all the meal, gave a big burp, then nestled against Spence's shoulder.

Spence felt the tiny mouth move against his neck as if the baby was giving him a kiss. He smiled at the idea. If his bachelor friends could see him now.

After changing Nick's diaper, he picked up Hannah, who had managed to suck on her fingers while he fed her twin. Repeating his success with Nick, he let her suck his finger while they went to the kitchen.

Back in the bedroom, he sat in the rocker and fed Hannah. Her eyes locked on his face while she ate. Her expression was one of absolute trust.

A funny, achy pang shot through him. He found himself wanting to be worthy of that open, candid gaze. He remembered another night and another girl looking at him with eyes as blue as the sea, with trust in her gaze.

"I'll never let anyone hurt you," he said to the tiny girl on an impulse he didn't understand but couldn't deny. He wasn't sure why he felt compelled to make the promise.

Hannah stopped sucking and smiled up at him, dazzling him with the purity of her faith.

Spence recalled an eleven-year-old and the way she had trusted him from the moment they'd met.

He'd let her down when he'd imposed sex on their friendship. He'd lost his best friend that night. Ally had been distant with him from that moment on.

Hannah's eyes drifted closed and she stopped nursing. He changed her and laid her in the bassinet. She didn't stir at all. Nick, too, slept peacefully.

Spence looked at the clock. Four in the morning. Man, he was beat. He returned to the living room, lifted Ally's feet and tucked them against his hip as he took his place. He slumped into the comfy cushions and closed his eyes. He'd rest for just a moment....

Ally woke and listened intently. She must have been dreaming. Someone had called her name—

"Ally?"

She sat up on the sofa just as Rose walked into the room. A big smile lit the other woman's face.

"Well, so here you two are," Rose said.

Spence stirred and opened his eyes. Ally stared at him in horror. They had both been asleep. On the sofa. Together.

"The twins," she said, worried that something might have happened to them while she'd slept deeply and peacefully, snuggled against Spence's warm body, her head on one arm of the sofa, his on the opposite end. She leaped off the sofa and hugged the afghan against her.

"They're fine. I looked in on the dears." She peered closely at Ally. "You have odd speckles in your hair."

Ally looked at her mother-in-law in confusion.

"She painted one of the bedrooms yesterday," Spence informed his mom.

"Oh, yes. I'd forgotten." Ally looked out the window at the bright July sunshine. "What day is this?"

Rose laughed. "Sunday. The days blur together when you're not getting any sleep, don't they?"

Ally nodded, then looked at Spence. "Did the babies wake up again in the night?"

"Yeah. I fed and changed them. They went right back to sleep," he answered.

"Oh."

"That's good," Rose spoke up, beaming at her son. "Ally needed the rest." She gave Ally a stern glance. "You really shouldn't be doing extra work now. The twins will need all your energy."

"I know. I wanted to get one of the rooms ready so that I could move Hannah into it. They wake each other up when they cry."

"Hmm, you probably should leave them together." Rose paused and considered. "In fact, it might be a good idea for them to sleep in the same bed since they're used to being close to each other. Where're the baby beds we ordered?"

"In the garage, still in the cartons. I haven't put them together yet. I was waiting for the rooms to be ready."

"Put a clock under the mattress," Rose continued. "They could hear their mother's heartbeat in the womb, and the sound will be soothing."

"I hadn't thought about that," Ally confessed. "It wasn't in any of the child-psychology books,

either. In fact, I've found very little from my studies that compares to the reality of having babies in the house.'' Her smile was wry.

''Isn't that the truth?'' Rose agreed. ''I brought homemade cinnamon rolls over. Why don't you take a shower while I make coffee?''

''There're eggs and bacon in the fridge. In case Spence wants something more substantial,'' Ally said.

''Sounds good.'' He took the afghan from her and folded it neatly before placing it on the sofa again. ''Don't use all the hot water,'' he admonished Ally. ''I could use a shower, too. Then I'll look at the baby beds.''

''I'll hurry,'' she promised and proceeded to do so. She was out and dressed in fifteen minutes.

While he showered, she dried her hair and pinned it on top of her head. That would keep it off her neck and out of the way. Wearing old jeans and a T-shirt, her feet in sandals, she hurried to the kitchen to help Rose with breakfast, aware that Spence was in her shower. That fact caused confusion inside her. She couldn't figure out why.

The twins slept until the adults sat down to breakfast. Ally paused with her fork in midair at the first yell.

''Great timing,'' Spence said with a grin. ''Come on. I'll show you a new trick I learned last night...well, in the wee hours of the morning,'' he said to Ally.

They wheeled the bassinets into the kitchen. Spence showed her how he'd plugged up Nick's

crying with his finger. "You need to get some of those fake things."

"Pacifiers. I think I got some at the baby shower. I hadn't intended to use them. Wait." She dashed into the nursery, checked a drawer and found two pacifiers that had been tied to a gift package. She hurried back to the kitchen. "Found them."

After washing them, she and Spence offered them to the twins. Hannah took to it at once. Nick spit his out.

"Yeah, I know, fella. It isn't as good as the real thing, but you gotta learn to take what you can get—"

"Spencer McBride," Rose said sternly.

He glanced at the two women, his grin unrepentant. "Sorry. I'll forget the avuncular advice for now. When he's a teenager, I'll tell him about the birds and bees if you like," he volunteered to Ally, his eyes filled with humor.

Ally felt her temperature rise. "I'll think about it…in about sixteen years."

Rose laughed softly, with more than a hint of nostalgia. "It will pass before you know it. Kids go from climbing trees and Little League to dates and prom nights with hardly a pause."

Ally's gaze flicked to Spence. Their eyes locked for a second. She was suddenly sure he was remembering graduation night and the dance neither had attended. Heat swept into her face and she looked away.

That memory seemed much too close all at once. It mingled with the fresh one from that morning, of

waking with a warm male body pressed along her length, her toes snuggled under his sheltering arm....

Heat spread from some tiny hidden spot deep inside her to all parts of her body. "I want to get pictures of everything, their first smile—"

"Sorry, I already got that. Hannah smiled at me last night, or this morning, as the case may be."

"That was probably a gas—"

"Babies know a lot more than we give them credit for," Rose broke in. She gave Ally a conspiratorial smile. "I think they can smile from the moment they're born. They just reserve them until they see if they have something to smile about. That's my theory, and I'm sticking to it."

Affection filled Ally. Rose was a wonderful person. Even though she'd grieved for the loss of her son, she'd been there for Ally through the aftermath of Jack's death. Although neither had mentioned guilt, Ally was sure Rose had known how terrible Ally had felt about not checking on Jack as soon as she got in and found he wasn't at home.

She was sorry Jack would never know the twins. He had seemed eager for children. Like Ally, perhaps he had thought having a family would cement their shaky marriage.

Pushing the sadness behind her, she tried to let the past go while she chatted and ate. The twins took in everything with their wise gazes and solemn little faces. By the time the adults finished the meal, her heart was easy, and she felt ready to face the future once more.

When she warmed the formula, Rose asked to feed one of the twins. Ally handed Hannah to her grandmother and lifted Nick into her arms a little fearfully.

He gazed at her the whole time he ate.

"He's decided you're okay," Spence murmured close to her ear. "We had a long talk about it during the wee hours of the morning."

"That's a relief." She spoke to Rose. "Poor Spence didn't know what he had walked into last night. The twins and I were all crying."

Rose made sympathetic sounds. "I was worried about you. Babies can be so hard on new mothers. That's why I asked Spence to come over when I, uh..."

"Got another migraine?" Spence suggested with an innocent air that didn't jibe with his assessing perusal of his mother.

"Yes, a migraine. That's what it was," Rose confirmed. "I used to have them a lot when I was younger."

Ally met Spence's eyes. Both of them were worried. Rose had never been sick with more than a cold in years that either of them recalled. A tremor of unease ran down her nerves. How would she ever manage without Rose's calm advice and soothing presence? She really would be alone to raise the twins if something happened to the older woman.

"Maybe you should make an appointment with the doctor and get a checkup," she suggested in a neutral tone.

"I will."

Spence glanced at his watch. "I'm helping Johnny finish up the sprinkler controls today. I'd better run. I'll be over later to set up the cribs." He kissed his mom on the cheek and tapped Ally on the shoulder. "Sleep every chance you get," he ordered.

"I feel perfectly rested, thanks to you."

"Five hours is hardly a full night. Make her take a nap," he said to his mom.

After he left, Rose laid the sleeping Hannah in the bassinet. "Spence would make such a good father."

Ally nodded, not trusting herself to speak.

"He'll make a wonderful husband, too," Rose had said.

Chapter Five

He'll make a wonderful husband.

The idea, once spoken, was very hard to get out of her mind, Ally realized as Sunday passed slowly. As usual, the twins settled into sleep as soon as the sun came up.

At noon, she woke them for their baths, then played with them on a quilt on the floor before feeding them and putting them back to bed. She read the paper after that.

Lying on the sofa, she remembered Spence's warm presence there when she woke that morning. His feet had been tucked into the corner behind her head. Her feet had been snug against him, his arm draped casually over her legs.

Before she could drift into a nap, she heard a car

engine in the drive. Her heart beat hard at the thought of Spence returning. She sternly told the errant organ to behave itself and went to the door.

It was him.

"Hi. I didn't know if you had a toolbox, so I brought mine just in case," he said, hefting a red metal box out of the trunk of his car. "You said the beds were in the garage?"

"Yes. Against the back wall. The door is unlocked."

He pushed the roll-up door out of the way with an easy show of strength. Ally went to the kitchen and opened the connecting door so she could watch and still be able to hear if the twins woke.

"The kids still sleeping?" he asked as he removed crib parts from a carton.

"Yes."

"I'm no expert, but maybe you should try to keep them awake during the day so they'll sleep at night." He paused to cast her a questioning glance over his shoulder. "Or is that against the baby-book rules?"

"I don't know. I'm not sure there are any rules. One of my clients said she fed her kids a thin cereal as soon as she brought them home and they slept all night from the first, but Claire didn't think that was a good idea. Their digestive systems may not be ready for solids. They could develop allergies."

She stopped, realizing she was telling him more than he could possibly want to know about babies.

"Allergies can be dangerous," he agreed while

fitting two pieces together. "Can you hold this bar while I bolt it to the headboard?"

She held the pieces firmly in place while he slipped washers on, then fastened them with a thick bolt. His hands brushed hers as he worked. His arm pressed against hers. Once his hair tickled her chin as he bent forward to line up the holes for another bolt.

She inhaled the scent of his shampoo and talc and the subtle essence of his warmth. She thought of his heat along her back on the sofa that morning. Longing wended its way through her, a quiet nostalgia for something she sensed she'd missed in life but couldn't describe.

When he looked up, their eyes met and held. She saw his pupils widen. Awareness entered into those dark, mysterious depths. She couldn't breathe. Neither could she tear her gaze from his.

"Ally," he said in a husky tone.

She blinked and looked away. "What do we do next?" she asked brightly, bending over the crib.

"Hold this while I fit the end in place," he ordered. "Mmm, this spring must go somewhere. When all else fails, read the instructions."

He flashed her a smile, then checked the sketch to see how the parts went together. Watching his dark head bent over the drawings, she recalled how they had worked on projects together in the past. She tried to remember something she and Jack had done together, but they had never shared that type of camaraderie.

The need to cry rose in her so suddenly she was

shocked by it. She bit down on the inside of her lip until the moment passed. The past was gone. All of it.

When they got the bed together, he eyed the doorway from the garage into the kitchen. "That looks like a tight squeeze," he murmured.

His gaze flicked to her, laying down a trail of heat from her breasts to someplace deep inside. She swallowed as desire overcame the odd sadness. She didn't know what was wrong with her today.

"I forgot the door," she admitted. "I think the bed is wider."

He cocked one dark eyebrow at her. "Are you saying I have to take this apart, then get it inside before setting it up?"

"The carpenter said something about the doors being narrow. He had trouble getting some of his stuff inside. I had forgotten about it until now."

Spence shook his head, but he was smiling. "Well, let's give it a try."

Lifting at each end, they eased the bed through the door with a hair's breadth on each side.

"I hope the door to the other room isn't off by a quarter inch, or we'll never make it through," he said.

"I can put it in my room if we need to."

"Lucky kids," Spence murmured, his gaze once more roaming over her jeans and T-shirt.

Heat rushed to all parts of her body. She thought of him there with her. Sharing her bed. Confused, she glanced away from his enticing looks.

"What?" he asked softly.

"Nothing." She decided the better part of valor was ignoring his teasing remark. He surely hadn't meant it the way she had taken it. "We can leave the crib in the living room for a while. I was thinking of trying Rose's idea of putting them together for a few days."

"And don't forget the clock."

"Right. I have an old wind-up one I used in college."

"Which you probably bought secondhand."

"Yes. At the Goodwill store, actually."

She saw his smile widen. She'd been very frugal during her youth, but she had refused to accept gifts from him or his family. She had wanted to be a friend, not a charity case. She still felt that way, she realized.

"A man likes a wife who'll be careful with their money. Okay, let's go." He picked up one end of the crib.

Ally walked backward, carrying her end of the load while they made their way into the living room. She found herself wondering what else he wanted in a wife.

"Against the wall," she directed.

After putting the crib in position, Spence headed purposefully down the hall. She followed, curious. He opened the door at the end of the hall and went inside.

"This the paint?" He indicated the cans on the floor.

"Yes. Both bedrooms are white. I'm going to use curtains in the same pattern for each room. And a

border print when the paint is dry. Nick's has red fire engines on it while Hannah's has kittens.''

"Sexist."

"What?"

"Fire engines for boys, kittens for girls," he admonished. "I'm pretty sure that's sexist."

She propped her hands on her hips and went into a defensive mode. "What would you suggest?"

"Ducks."

"Ducks?" she repeated as if she'd never heard of them. "Why ducks?"

"Why not? You could do fish if you don't like ducks."

"I'll take your suggestion under advisement."

He checked the cans of paint. "I suppose the curtains are pink for Hannah and blue for Nick."

"No," she responded icily. "They are both plaid and in primary colors, for your information. I'm using lots of colors in each room. Bright colors are considered good for children's development. Studies have shown they are as attracted to them as adults are."

Spence stacked the cans neatly in the center of the room. "Whatever you say, doc."

He shot her a laughing glance. She realized he'd been giving her a hard time on purpose. She sighed. "I need to lighten up. I've been so tense lately."

"Babies do that to a person."

"How do you know so much about it?" she challenged.

"I've had lots of chances to observe parents and babies since moving back to Buttonwood. It seems

every couple in town is having one. Or two," he added.

She trailed after him into the next room. He examined the stack of baseboards. He was in shorts, as usual. His legs were long and tanned and rippled with muscles as he checked the boards for flaws.

"Romance adds its own confusion and tension, too. Johnny was hard to deal with while he and Claire got sorted out. Thank God it didn't take long."

Ally was rather taken aback by this casual observation from a confirmed bachelor. "I didn't think men noticed things like that unless it was on instant replay during the Super Bowl game."

"Oh, we notice." He glanced around. "Where's the paint roller?"

"In the garage. Why?"

"I'll finish the painting. It shouldn't take more than three or four hours."

A picture of Spence and a woman, working together on a house, leaped into her mind. She couldn't see the woman clearly, but the image made her uneasy.

Because he was with a woman? Or because she wanted to be the woman?

He'll make a wonderful husband.

Oh, how she wished Rose hadn't said those words. They were going to haunt her the rest of her life.

"Famous last words," she managed to scoff in a light tone at his boast. "Have you ever painted before?"

He rose slowly and turned toward her, his eyes narrowed dangerously. "Are you questioning my abilities, woman?"

"Yes."

Puffing his chest out, he assumed the posture of an arrogant male. "Oh, ye of little faith, you'll pay for those words. Let's see, what shall the forfeit be when I do a perfect job in four hours?"

"Ha, it'll never happen."

He snapped his fingers. "A week of home-cooked meals if I don't finish before six."

"It's a bet as long as I get the same if you don't finish—but with you doing the cooking."

"Done."

He held out his hand. She hesitated, then slipped her hand in his. They shook on it.

"Spread the drop cloth, will you?" he asked, heading for the door. "I'll get the other stuff from the garage."

"Can't. That would be cheating. Three hours and fifty-nine minutes to go," she announced, looking at her watch.

He cast her a mock glare, then strode out to fetch the supplies. She spread the sheets of plastic the carpenters had left, then frowned as she realized what she'd done. Win or lose, Spence would be over at her house every night for a week.

Taking pity on him and feeling more than a tad guilty about letting him do the work, she helped by cutting in around the windows and doors. When the children woke, she stopped and cared for them,

plugging up Hannah, as Spence called it, with the pacifier while Nick ate.

"Just like a man," she murmured to the baby. "You guys have to have attention first. From now on, we take turns. You hear?"

Nick stopped sucking. She tried to decide if he was really smiling or having a gas bubble. A gas bubble, she decided when he burped. She laughed softly and walked down the hall. At the doorway, she stopped and watched Spence move the paint roller in firm, quick strokes across the new walls.

He'd taken off his shirt. His skin was tanned and smooth, with only a sprinkling of hair over his lean torso.

It seemed impossible that she had once touched him and stroked her hands over him, that they had once kissed each other passionately. That had been so long ago.

He was a handsome man, not in a pretty-boy way, but with a rugged masculinity that combined grace and strength. She wondered why no woman had ever snared him, then recalled that he had lived for a short time with someone when he moved to Durango after law school. But like all his romances, the relationship hadn't lasted long.

Could there be some dark secret flaw in him that she had never seen?

To her, he had always been a hero—brave and loyal and honorable. Maybe other women didn't see him that way. Maybe they saw the charmer who moved from woman to woman and didn't linger

long with any of them. Maybe Spence hadn't married because he wasn't good husband material.

Rose's words echoed in her mind. Of course Rose saw him differently. Mothers always did see their sons as perfect.

Ally smiled at Nick and kissed him on the forehead. "You're perfect to me," she whispered. "Even if you are a handful for a new mom."

Through the door, Spence glanced her way, then stopped and watched her and Nick for a long minute. Something shifted inside her as his expression softened.

"Madonna and Child," he said. "Someone should paint a picture of you two at this moment."

She was touched by his words. Longing spiraled through her. She wished...she wished...

Hearing a cry from the bedroom, she was spared from finishing that thought. Hurrying to Hannah, she tended the other child, then played with both babies by singing nursery rhymes to them until they fell asleep.

When she returned to the new rooms, she found Spence had completed one wall. "You're fast."

"And how," he said, giving her a sexy glance and waggling his eyebrows at her.

She laughed and took up her brush once more. By the time she finished around the window sills and door frames, he was done with the last wall. It was five after five.

"Let's see...for dinner tonight, I'll take a steak and those twice-baked potatoes you do so well."

"You haven't cleaned up the roller yet," she reminded him. "Cleanup goes with the deal."

"There's plenty of time." He picked up the last can of paint. "I'll touch up some places you missed in the other room." He ambled into the second bedroom. "Hey," he called, "you haven't even started in the bathroom."

"I know," she replied dryly.

"We'll do it tomorrow. Leave it until I get here. That's an order." He stuck his head around the door frame and gave her a stern frown.

She saluted with the brush. "Right, captain."

After they had taken turns showering, he insisted on going out for fried chicken rather than letting her cook. She promised him the steak dinner the following night.

"See you around six," he said as he left.

Watching the ten o'clock news, she wondered if this was wise. Spence would make a wonderful male role model for the kids, but she would have to be careful. Again she didn't voice the source of her worry or what exactly she should be careful about, but she instinctively knew there was danger in wanting too much from life.

"Go to bed."

Ally returned Spence's glare and shook her head. "I can nap during the day."

"Yeah? Like you did when you painted that room?"

"This is a ridiculous quarrel."

"You got that right."

He took a deep breath and Ally prepared herself for his oh-so-reasonable tone, the one that implied she was the stubborn moron in this crowd.

"Look," he said. "You sleep until midnight while I watch the kids. Tomorrow's Saturday and I can sleep in. That way we both get some rest."

"It's only eight o'clock. I'm not sleepy."

"You were yawning your head off while we ate."

She couldn't dispute that. She was tired. The twins had been fussy all week. Nick had spit up his formula regularly, requiring frequent changes of clothing as well as bedding, so she hadn't put them in the crib. The pediatrician had advised trying another brand.

Spence gave her a relentless appraisal. She knew every hour of missed rest was reflected in the circles under her eyes. She didn't exactly look her best.

Tension ran along her nerves like little stray electrical currents. "This isn't a good idea," she started, then stopped abruptly as she realized the direction she was going.

He studied her for a long five seconds. "What isn't?"

A joke seemed the best way out. "Your being here, helping out all the time the way you have this week. I...we...the twins and I will start expecting it and then you'll be sorry when we demand all your time and energy. You won't have time for those swinging singles parties at the apartment complex."

Instead of smiling, he frowned ominously. The tension soared in the kitchen, which was where they were having the argument. She wished she hadn't mentioned his bachelor life. It was none of her business.

His eyes narrowed. "I'll decide how my time is best spent. Being with my niece and nephew seems pretty important to me. They'll need a male influence in their lives. Or do you think swinging bachelors aren't responsible enough—"

His scathing remarks were cut short by a knock on the kitchen door. Rose bustled in.

"Hi, you two. I just got in from work and saw Spence's car here. I stopped by the bakery and bought a strawberry pie. I figured you needed a treat."

"Thank you. That was kind," Ally said, disconcerted as Rose's sharp glance traveled from one to the other. "I'll get plates. We can share it."

"You were working late tonight," Spence said to his mom when they were seated around the table. "Anything wrong?"

"No. I was just getting ahead so I could take tomorrow off." She patted Ally's arm. "I thought I would stay with the twins tonight and let Ally catch up on her sleep."

A vast relief poured through Ally. "That would be wonderful. Spence and I were discussing that—"

"We were having a flaming fight," he corrected.

"I noticed," Rose said with a smile for both of them. "I don't think you should ignore Spence's

offer,'' she told Ally. ''Twenty-four-hour care of two babies is too hard on one person. Don't be too proud to accept our help.''

Spence ate the last bite of his pie and leaned back in his chair with a satisfied smile. ''Yeah, don't be so proud.''

Ally wondered if everyone thought she was incapable of taking care of the twins. Maybe they thought she shouldn't have taken them, since she was alone now....

Or perhaps she was being overly sensitive. ''I'm not proud. I just didn't want to impose.''

''We're family,'' Rose chided gently. ''Of course you can impose. That's what families are for.''

Ally didn't say anything to that. Until her parents had died, she'd believed that to be true, but not anymore. Fate could be less than kind, she'd discovered.

Spence glanced at his watch. ''Guess I'll be off. There's this wild party I was invited to...'' His voice trailed off with a mocking tone.

''As I'd suspected,'' Ally shot right back. ''Friday night and he tried to tell me he didn't have anything better to do than baby-sit. Yeah, right.''

He rose and stretched. ''Johnny and I will be here tomorrow afternoon to start on the baseboards. You might invite Claire over. You women can compare notes on babies while we work. I thought I might grill hamburgers for supper for all of us. If you don't mind.''

''Well, no, I mean, of course I don't mind.''

''Do that baked-bean dish,'' Spence requested of

Ally. "The one you said your mom used to fix. Okay?"

Ally nodded.

"That sounds nice." Rose smiled approvingly. "I have bridge club tomorrow. It's at Blanche's house, so I'll be able to tell you all the latest gossip."

Spence chuckled, said good-night and left.

"Speaking of gossip, everyone is wondering who's the father of Rachel Arquette's baby. Has she said anything to you?" Ally asked the older woman when they were alone.

"No. She's one of my best nurses. I hope she doesn't leave after the birth." Rose frowned. "I've discounted the rumors about the father."

"I heard it might be Dennis Reid." Ally propped her chin on her hand and considered. "She was dating Colt Rollins before he left for that new federal inoculation program in New Mexico. I thought she was in love with him."

"Dennis is sort of hinting that it's his." Rose shook her head. "I hope not. He's a pain in the— Well, never mind. Just because he's a dirty rotten skunk who tries to undermine my running of the clinic doesn't mean he isn't a wonderful person."

Ally joined in the laughter. She didn't care for Dr. Reid, either. She, too, had had a couple of run-ins with him over patients' care. He thought people used psychology as a crutch to excuse themselves for their problems. She thought he wanted to prescribe a pill for every situation, warranted or not, and get on to the next patient.

"I wonder if Colt knows," Ally said. "Rachel should tell him."

"Assuming it's his."

"Yes." Ally picked up the used pie plates and took them to the sink. "I'm sure Blanche, as the official town gossip, will have an exact count on how many people think the baby is Dr. Reid's and how many think it is Dr. Rollins's."

"There's probably a betting pool among the interns at the hospital. I heard they had one last week on how long it would take to perform a quadruple heart bypass."

Ally grinned. "The nurses had one at the clinic on whether Dr. Davis and Johnny Winterhawk would tie the knot after they got involved over the baby that was left on his doorstep."

"I'm sure there was a lot of speculation on the paternity of that child."

"Yes. I'm glad things worked out for them. I saw them in the park not long ago. They looked very happy."

"A charming family," Rose agreed. She sighed. "I worry about Spence. I thought he would marry before Jack. He was always the most outgoing of my boys. And the most nurturing. We had a procession of injured animals and lonely children through our home during his youth. Did you notice how natural he is with the twins?"

"Yes." Ally finished washing up their few dishes. "I think I'll try to sleep now. Call if you need me."

"I will. Don't worry about a thing." Rose shooed her from the room.

In her bedroom, Ally slipped into a summer gown of crinkled cotton, but she didn't go to sleep immediately.

She had been one of the lonely children Spence had brought home for his mom to "fix." Rose had accepted her into their lives in her bighearted way. She'd let Ally help cook meals and had assigned her a turn at washing dishes just as she had with Jack and Spence. The chores had made a lonely child feel welcome and needed.

Pressing a hand to her heart, Ally struggled with her idealized memories of the past and the reality of it. Spence's family had been kind to her, but she didn't like thinking of herself as a stray to be taken in. For some reason, that hurt.

Again she found herself wondering if she'd married Jack because she'd loved his family. No, she'd loved him, too. Maybe not in that breathless, heart-achy way one sees in books and movies, but with a tenderness that had been real. She didn't regret their marriage.

Unbidden, the memory of that moonlit night of passion with Spence flooded her mind. Her breath caught and pangs of longing coursed through her. She hadn't felt such wild desire since then. At times, that had worried her.

But it had been an adolescent thing, she reminded herself. A mad infatuation that had evaporated in the light of day. She'd gotten past all that.

She was a mother now, with two adorable children to raise. As soon as they started sleeping all night, she was going to enjoy her little family!

Chapter Six

Ally was nervous as she prepared seven-layer dip for the corn chips on Saturday afternoon. The hamburgers were patted out and in a covered bowl in the refrigerator, ready to go on the grill. The salad was made.

From the additional rooms to the cottage, she could hear periodic banging as Spence and Johnny hammered the baseboards and window trim into place. The work appeared to be going more slowly than they had anticipated.

Maybe that was because of smashed thumbs and fingers. Each male had been in the kitchen for an ice cube to soothe an aching joint that afternoon.

Spence appeared in the kitchen.

"What's funny?" he demanded, looking hot and

irked and sexier than any man had the right to be, dressed as he was in a pair of ragged cutoffs, old sneakers that should have been recycled into something useful long ago and no shirt.

"You'd get mad if I told you."

He paused with one hand on the refrigerator door. "Yeah? Now you have to tell me."

His eyes took on a devilish gleam she recognized from their long-lost youth. That gleam always appeared when he wanted information out of her or one of their friends. He could be cajoling or demanding, whatever the occasion called for.

"Well," she said, drawing the moment out just as she had back in those days, "I was wondering if my insurance covered inept friends, who volunteered over my objections, for injuries."

He glared at her through narrowed eyes. "Inept, huh? You'll eat those words, Miss Doubting Thomasina, when you see how great we're doing."

"I saw those planks that were sawed off, then laid aside while another was measured and redone."

He took two long steps and was suddenly in her face. "Okay, so it took us a couple of tries to catch on to angling the cut to fit the corners. So fire us," he mock-challenged, holding his mouth in a severe line.

"I would, but you're all that's available. And you're cheap," she added wryly.

"True, but I have a strategy." He assumed a wise mien. "You'll owe me big-time after all the

work I've put in. And I intend to collect, probably for years.''

She grinned at him, feeling lighthearted and happy all at once. "Like how?''

''Home-cooked meals, for a start. I'd like more of those.''

''After a week of my cooking? Jack preferred to eat out as often as possible.''

The gleam left his eyes. ''I don't give a damn about Jack and your relationship with him.''

A heaviness entered her chest. ''You never approved of my marriage to him, did you?''

Spence's face set in forbidding lines that she had rarely seen in him. He looked angry, dangerous, the male animal roused to fury.

Or maybe she imagined that flash of temperament as it disappeared in an instant, replaced by the usual sardonic manner she had grown accustomed to during the past ten years.

''I wouldn't have thought my brother was the man for you, but your marriage was none of my business,'' he stated in an offhand manner and walked off.

After retrieving two sodas from the fridge, he returned to the room where work was in progress. Ally tried to assess what had just passed between them.

She had sensed Spence's disapproval of the marriage—no one could be as close as they had once been and not recognize the other's body language, no matter what words they spoke—but now it was out in the open.

Pride made her keep her head up and continue with her preparations for dinner. Claire and little Lucy were supposed to be over soon.

Thirty minutes later, two things happened at once. The doorbell rang and both babies started crying.

Ally didn't know which to attend to first.

"You get the door. I'll handle the twins," Spence said, hurrying up the hallway to the nursery.

"Thanks."

She rushed to the front door. "Claire, please come in. Here, let me help you," she said in a quiet tone, seeing that Claire's baby was asleep. She took the diaper bag that had slipped from the pediatrician's shoulder. She peered at the sleeping baby in the infant seat. "Oh, look how big your Lucy is. She's what—three months old now?"

"Four. She's nearly doubled her weight and grown an inch since we got her. The asthma is under control."

"Spence said she's sleeping all night, too." Ally heard the envy in her voice and grimaced. No one liked a whiner, she reminded herself sternly.

Claire sent her a sympathetic smile. "Rose mentioned the twins have their days and nights mixed up. They'll get it straight soon. Have you tried keeping them awake for a while in the evenings, then feeding them before putting them to bed?"

"I tried it a couple of times, but I was feeding them first. I'll try it the other way next time."

"That might give you four or five hours of rest, maybe six if they have a good feeding."

"That would be a relief." She led the way into the living room. "Do you want to put Lucy to bed in here? I have a crib you can use." She pointed out the crib next to the wall that Spence had set up for her.

"Thanks. I'll leave her in the infant seat. She likes sleeping in it." She set the infant seat in the crib, then followed Ally to the kitchen. "Did you change Nicholas's formula?"

"Yes," a masculine voice answered. "He's doing better."

Spence entered the kitchen, pushing the bassinets in front of him. Both babies looked around with interest. Nick had a pacifier in his mouth.

"Well, you certainly look right at home," Claire teased Spence. "Johnny and I will have to keep you in mind when we need a baby-sitter. How much do you charge?"

"More than you can afford," he assured the other woman.

"He's dirt cheap," Ally insisted.

Claire looked from one to the other. "Or maybe he only makes his services available to certain people. How does one get on his good side?" she demanded.

"Oh, there are ways," Spence told her, "but I'm not telling." His gaze flicked to Ally, then back to the twins.

There was a dangerous undercurrent in the conversation, but Ally couldn't say what it was or why she felt that way. It seemed that Spence was speak-

ing on some level beyond the wry humor he displayed.

"You need any help feeding these two?" he asked.

Ally shook her head.

"I can help, too," Claire volunteered.

"Nick doesn't like to be fussed over," Spence informed them. "He's a straightforward kind of person. Good eats, a warm bath, a snug bed and he's happy."

Ally couldn't let that pass. "Who was up, walking him around and showing him the stars, at two a.m. a couple of nights ago?" she demanded.

"That was a guy thing. You women wouldn't get it."

Claire burst out laughing. So did Ally.

Spence gave them a superior glance, then grinned and headed back to the addition where the hammering had started again.

Ally fed Nick while Claire took care of Hannah. Lucy woke soon after that. The women talked while the babies observed the scene in their wise way.

"I had something strange happen this week," Claire said at one point.

"Oh?" Ally mixed a vinaigrette dressing for the salad and set out a veggie platter to munch on.

"Do you know Dr. Reid, chief of staff at the clinic?"

"Yes."

"He signed Rachel Arquette and himself up for Lamaze classes."

"Ah. So he is the father," Ally deduced.

"Well, this is what's odd. Rachel removed Dennis's name. Then Colt Rollins—"

"Oh, is he back from that government program he volunteered for out in New Mexico?"

"Uh-huh."

"I've been totally out of touch since I brought the twins home."

"Babies do that to a person," Claire said ruefully. "But listen to this and tell me what you think. Colt signed himself up to take the classes with Rachel."

"Do both men think they're the father?"

"Apparently."

"Hmm. Rachel never struck me as that kind of person," Ally admitted. "I don't know her all that well, but from what I've seen of her at the hospital, she seems very nice. Rose says she's tops as a nurse. I can't see her involved with two men at the same time."

"It's really a mystery—"

The doorbell stopped the conversation. Ally answered it. "Well, hello," she said in surprise.

The sheriff stood on the small porch. He removed a toothpick from the corner of his mouth and stuck it in his pocket. "Hi, doc," he said in his friendly way.

Three years her senior, Hank Wright had been the second person Ally had met after moving to Buttonwood. His outgoing manner, coupled with a friendly appreciation of the opposite sex, always put her at ease around the lawman.

"What brings you out this way?"

"I was just going off duty when I got a call about a disturbance out this way. I told the dispatcher I'd answer it since it was on my way home."

"Oh? I haven't heard of anything."

"That's probably because you're the disturbance."

She stared at him in confusion. Footsteps approached from behind her. She recognized Spence's stride.

"Hey, Hank, what's happening?" he asked.

"Answering a call. Seems you people have been making a lot of noise and carrying on something awful over here."

Realization dawned on Ally. "That had to have been Mrs. Snells. She doesn't like children. She's reported me for every infraction she could think of for years."

"You did steal those apples off her tree that time," Spence reminded her solemnly. He turned to Hank. "I tried to keep her from a life of crime—"

"You fibber!" Ally appealed to Hank. "Spence was the one who said she'd given permission for us to help ourselves to her wormy old apples."

Hank grinned. "This time she says you're disturbing her rest. It's Sunday, and you're not supposed to be making all that racket."

"Johnny and I are trying to finish the addition on Ally's house for the twins' bedrooms," Spence explained, gesturing down the hall. "The carpenter was injured and will be out of commission for a while."

Ally was aware of him standing right behind her, his bare chest brushing her shoulder as he talked to the lawman.

"I handled the accident involving Jim and his son. The old man got a pretty bad leg break. What are you and Johnny doing?"

Hank followed Spence down the hall and into the new rooms. Ally listened to them discuss the work for a minute, then returned to the kitchen and told Claire about the lawman's visit due to her neighbor's complaint.

"That old meany," Claire said in annoyance. "Did you know she used to teach first grade? My mother had her. She said she would never send one of us kids to Mrs. Snells's class. It would be cruel and unusual punishment."

"I agree. Let's see, I have enough baked beans and hamburgers, but I'd better make more salad. Hank will probably stay for dinner. The last I saw, he was taking off his gun and preparing to show the other two how to cut mitered corners."

Ally's prediction was accurate. At seven, the men called it a day, washed up and trooped in to be fed. Later, seated around the table, talking and laughing with the three men and Claire, it came to her that this was what life was about—sharing moments like this with friends.

Not a terribly outgoing person herself, during her marriage she had practically become a recluse, withdrawing more and more into her work. With hindsight, she saw this as a way of coping—and not facing the problems in the marriage.

Spence had been right. She should never have married Jack. They didn't complement each other's talents and basic traits. The sadness that had lived in her for the past eight months washed over her.

A hand touched hers under cover of the table. She glanced up. Spence removed his hand, but continued to study her with eyes that saw too much.

She smiled and jumped to her feet. "Ready for dessert? We have chocolate or cherry pie. Since you men have done such excellent work, you may have both if you prefer."

Hank smiled broadly. "Ah, a woman after my own heart," he declared.

"Forget it," Spence said. "She has two kids to raise. She can't be wasting her time on the likes of you."

Ally couldn't decide if she should be insulted or not.

After dessert and coffee, the Winterhawks packed up Lucy and left. Hank lingered, chatting with Spence about a case in which the lawman had been a witness for the D.A.'s office. The prime suspect had gotten off on a technicality.

"After all the work we put in breaking up that rustling ring, he gets off scot-free," Hank said in disgust.

She only half listened. It was peaceful, sitting there on the sofa with the vibrant sounds of male voices wafting around her as the stars came out and the sky darkened to indigo. She suppressed a yawn, then another.

"I think it's time for Ally to rest," Spence said,

seeing her cover another yawn. "She hasn't slept much since the kids arrived."

Besides, he didn't like the way Hank was eyeing her, as if she was a particularly tasty morsel. The sheriff was a good guy, but he had an eye for pretty women. Ally looked especially attractive tonight in a blue, summery outfit that showed off her delicate curves and lithe body.

Hank jumped to his feet. "I should have gone home hours ago."

He beamed a high-powered smile at Ally—which made Spence feel like socking him in his perfectly straight teeth—and took her hand when she stood.

"Dinner was great, the company was delightful," Hank complimented his hostess, "and those two bozos you had working for you needed a lot of help."

"I'm glad you stopped by," she said, flashing her own bright smile at the lawman.

Spence hid his impatience for the man to be gone.

She nodded toward Spence. "And thanks for not arresting my workers, such as they are, for disturbing the peace. What will you say in your report? Do you have to tell Mrs. Snells you stopped by?"

"I'll report that you're doing construction and the noise is a necessary adjunct to that. Also that the work should be finished in a week or so. With my help."

"Johnny and I were doing fine on our own," Spence said.

"Yeah? What about all those boards that were cut wrong?" Hank challenged.

Spence knew when to back off gracefully. "Okay, so we're on a learning curve." He held out his hand. "Thanks for helping us out."

Hank shook hands with him, then turned back to Ally and thanked her profusely for letting him stay for dinner.

"It was a pleasure," she said in her warm manner. "I'm grateful for your help."

"I'll stop by tomorrow afternoon. It's my early day, so I'll be free at two o'clock. Unless something comes up."

He managed to look the important, yet long-suffering, lawman at the same time. Spence gritted his teeth. At last, after more effusive words about dinner and the pleasure of her company, the man left.

Spence closed the door firmly after Hank. He glanced at his watch. "I suggest we get the twins up, play with them for a while, then feed them and see if they'll sleep for more than two hours."

"I can handle it," Ally assured him. "You don't have to stay. Rose helped out last night, so I had plenty of rest."

"Yeah, she told me. You woke up every time the kids did and insisted on feeding one while she did the other." He tapped her on the forehead. "We are family, you know. It's okay for us to help you out."

"I'm the one who wanted the babies. They're my responsibility."

"Stubborn," he muttered. When her chin tilted in a certain way, he couldn't help but smile. "Same ol' Ally."

She sighed, then laughed. "Yep, that's me, stubborn to the end. I'm going to finish cleaning the kitchen before the twins wake up. Do you want another cup of coffee?"

"Yes."

He ambled into the living room after her and gathered cups and used dessert plates. "You need a dishwasher," he said when they went into the kitchen.

She washed while he dried. "That's next on my list. I want to remodel the kitchen and update everything. It would be much more efficient with a breakfast bar across the middle and cabinets under that. Then this side would be the dining area."

"Hmm, new oak cabinets would look good. I saw some in the hardware store. You can order them and put them up yourself. It's cheaper that way."

"I'll discuss it with the carpenter when he recovers."

Her tone was repressive, and he wished he hadn't said the final words. He had no idea of her financial situation or if she could afford oak cabinets or not. In spite of all the years he'd known her, he realized he knew very little about her life now. Ally tended to be a private person.

Once she'd shared her secrets, her happiness, her every worry, with him. Once.

"Can you afford it?" he asked bluntly, suddenly determined not to be left out.

She rinsed the last saucer and put it in the drain basket. He picked it up and wiped it with the drying towel, which was getting pretty soggy. He hung it on the oven door handle to dry after putting the saucer on the shelf. He didn't think she was going to answer his nosy question.

Finally she glanced at him with an ironical smile. "Of course. Don't you know that all doctors, like all lawyers, are rich?"

"Oh, yeah. I forgot that for a moment."

He thought of the lucrative practice he'd given up to move back to Buttonwood. He would build it up again, but right now his income was less than it had been a year ago.

She filled his coffee cup with the last of the coffee, then washed the pot. Leaning against the counter, he watched her quick, efficient motions.

The insistent strum of sexual energy that had taunted him lately increased to a steady throb. He tried to look away from her, the source of countless nights of frustration in his past and in the present. It was no use.

She hung the dishcloth on the back of a cabinet door to dry, then turned to him, a dismissive smile in place. He didn't want to be dismissed, he discovered. He didn't want an argument about who went to bed and who didn't.

What exactly did he want?

The smile fled her mouth. A startled expression darted through her eyes, then she went very still.

He'd seen a doe and her fawn adopt that same still-ness when they'd sensed danger nearby.

He'd warned the deer by stepping out from be-hind a shrub and waving his arms. It looked like a warning was needed now.

"I want you," he said.

Her breath caught, and her mouth dropped open in a tiny gasp, then she was still again. He set the cup down and moved in on her, slowly, every movement controlled so as not to frighten.

"W-want?" she said, as if trying to figure out what the word meant.

"Yes."

He settled his hands on her shoulders, then, un-able to resist, lifted one to the sexy tangle of waves around her face. He clutched a handful of the silky tresses in his fist and leaned close. Her scent filled him with visions and made him dizzy with hot long-ing.

"Friendship be damned," he muttered. "I want you. In bed. Moving with me. As hot for me as I am for you."

"Spence!" Her voice was a croak of surprise.

"Shocked, Ally?" he said, taunting her as she had taunted him in every dream of his of late. "It's a natural state of affairs. Boy meets girl. Boy wants girl. Happens every day."

"But not to us," she reminded him. "We're friends. Sex destroys friendship."

He laughed sardonically. "What friendship? We haven't been friends for years. Not since that night

we didn't go to the prom, but parked in the moonlight instead.''

She watched him warily.

''I have often wondered what would have happened if we'd gone all the way that night, how our lives might have changed from that moment.''

''It would have been a mistake.''

Her certainty irked him.

''Why?''

''I…we…you explained it then—that we needed to stay friends. We had college and…and plans.''

She pressed her lips together. He remembered the wild kisses of that moonstruck night. And the one in the birthing room when the twins were born.

Heat slid through him, melting any notions of right and wrong, of playing fair, of keeping his distance.

He bent and claimed her mouth, experiencing the pleasure of her lips, which softened as shock passed through her again. He smiled slightly, then ran his tongue over the enticing sweetness to the treasure within.

She didn't resist.

His heart beat a rat-a-tat-tat against his ribs as she yielded and curved into him. He slipped one arm around her and gathered her close. He tugged gently on her hair, making the kiss harder, more demanding.

Flames licked at the edges of his conscience. He didn't care. What was right, what was honorable, suddenly seemed less important than this moment and the passion that burned fiercely between them.

When they both trembled with need, he turned and, propped against the counter, took her weight, opening his thighs so that she fit snugly against him. When she rubbed against the erection he couldn't hide, he tore his mouth from hers and rested his chin on her head, his eyes tightly closed as he sought control.

"As good as it gets," he murmured. "With you, it's always the best. Like that other time."

She shook her head, more in wonder than in denial of what he was saying. He knew that, although he didn't know how he knew it. He just did.

"We're adults," she whispered, "not kids. That's what's different this time."

"Yes."

He kissed her again. She gave him her mouth without hesitation. Hunger shot through him so fast, so hard, it was almost a pain.

"I've never wanted anyone the way I want you. Not in all the years since that night."

"That can't be true—"

"Yes," he said fiercely, anger rising as she tried to deny the intensity between them. "You know it, too. You feel it. If you're honest, you'll admit it."

She pulled away from him, anger invading the passion he saw in her eyes. He let her go but not without a fight with his inner self.

"I've always been honest with you. Just as you've been with me," she told him.

"Have we really?" he questioned. "All those years of your marriage, when we carefully avoided each other, was that honest?"

"It was honorable."

"Yes."

He didn't understand the bleakness that entered his soul. He didn't understand anything about his relationship with Ally at the moment. It was changing....

No. It *had* changed. In a instant. With the kiss and with the admission of the hunger.

Everything in him had shifted so that he no longer knew the landscape. Like the earth after a major quake that had brought down buildings, trees and mountains, all the familiar landmarks had disappeared and left him stranded in a morass of tangled images.

He hated confusion.

"You didn't feel anything like what we shared just now with Jack. Admit it. Be honest about that one thing," he demanded, not knowing why it was important that she do so. "Did you?"

She crossed her arms and backed up two steps. "So that's what this is all about."

Her voice dripped acid on his nerves. "What?" he asked.

"You always wanted to beat Jack. You two competed to be first, the best, the tallest, the smartest. Are you competing with Jack now by showing me what I missed when I chose him over you?"

Her words penetrated to the quick. He quelled the illogic of pained outrage and sought the cool reason of law. "There is no competition now. You're free. So am I. Are you afraid to follow up and see what happens between us?"

He laid the challenge directly at her feet. She promptly stomped on it.

"No. I have more important things to do than indulge in adolescent fantasy. I have the twins to raise."

She walked to the door, her back straight and stiff. "I can handle things here tonight. You can go."

He left before he did something he might regret. Then again, he might not have regrets come morning. He wasn't sure which would be worse.

Chapter Seven

Ally lay down on the leather sofa in her office, a baby tucked into either side. The three slept until her secretary woke them at two. It was time to get back to work. She put the twins in the playpen in the adjoining file storage room, made sure the clock on the floor under the playpen was ticking and returned to her office, closing the door silently behind her.

She yawned while she waited for her next appointment. Two weeks without a sound sleep made her yearn for hours of rest, with nothing to do but indulge herself.

Fat chance.

She rose to greet her next patient when the outer door opened. "Come in, Gary. How're you doing?"

"Fine."

The sixteen-year-old was one of her pro bono cases. She and the school counselor were trying to interest him in activities other than those of the gang of school dropouts he ran with. As a child from a dysfunctional family, he needed structure and acceptance. He got it from his gang.

"Feel like taking some tests today?" she asked.

He shrugged. "Sure."

She wasn't fooled by his nonchalance. He had an avid curiosity for all things scientific and was willing to participate if she explained exactly what they were doing.

"Today we're going to assess your interests. Did you know that everyone is born with natural dispositions that incline them to like one thing over another?"

"Yeah?"

"Yeah. We don't know why, but it's true. Personality is something you're born with. Character is what you make of it." She gave him a conspiratorial grin. "Let's find out what turns you on."

Interest lit up his dark gray eyes. He was a good-looking boy…young man, she amended. Gary was one of those kids who had never been young. Thanks to his alcoholic father, he'd often taken over the male role in his family. Like her, he'd mowed lawns, delivered papers and worked odd jobs to bring in additional money. He'd taken care of his mother and his younger sister as well as he could. Until he'd gotten mixed up with the gang, he'd had no support group.

Ally identified with his efforts. She'd had the McBride family when her life had taken a turn for the worse. Gary had no one.

She administered the battery of tests, carefully explaining what each one was supposed to disclose. Gary took them all enthusiastically, then asked a hundred questions as she went over his answers. Pleased, she'd told him he would have to give her a chance to study the results before she could answer all his queries.

When he left, Taylor arrived. Ally gave her a hug and asked about school.

"I'm through with finals and have a month off. I'm working two shifts at the diner so I can save more money for the fall semester. How it's going with you and the twins?"

"They're growing like weeds."

"Are they good?" Taylor asked. "You look tired."

"They're sleeping days and keeping me up at night, but I'm trying to get them out of that by keeping them awake more during the day. Dr. Davis says they'll soon get on a more reasonable schedule."

Ally led the way to the file room.

Taylor bent over the playpen. "They are pretty, aren't they?" she whispered.

"The most beautiful babies in the world."

The two women smiled at each other. Taylor's eyes clouded with tears. "I'm glad I heard you talking about adopting," she said. "They'll have the best home."

"I can't tell you how much I love them," Ally said sincerely. "And how grateful I am for this gift."

Ally observed Taylor as the girl gazed at the sleeping babies. Her biggest fear was that Taylor would take one look and decide she couldn't give them up. Ally swallowed a knot in her throat as she realized how hard it now would be for her to let them go.

Taylor sighed and said softly, "I did the right thing. For them. And for me. I'm glad that they have you and Rose. And Spence. He was nice during the birthing…a little embarrassed."

She giggled, sounding more like the carefree young student she should have been. Ally laughed, too, her fear easing up as Taylor gazed at the twins with pride and tenderness on her face, but with no signs of possessiveness. She realized the birth mother hadn't gone through the bonding process the way she and the children had during the past two weeks. Lots of bonding, she added with a smile. Two weeks worth. Fourteen sleepless nights.

"He's helped a lot with the twins since then," Ally said, remembering just how much he had done. "You've got to come out to the house. I've had two rooms added, one for each of the babies."

"That's good. I always wanted a room of my own. I had to share with two sisters." She rolled her eyes, indicating what a trial it had been.

Ally didn't point out how lucky she thought Taylor was, having a big family to love, even though they had been very poor. She pointed toward the

door, then tiptoed out of the file room, Taylor following right behind her.

They returned to the office. "Have a seat," Ally invited. "My next patient is late. We can talk until she arrives."

They chatted for a few minutes. When the buzzer sounded, announcing the next patient, Taylor left by the side door. "I'll be over at noon every day if that's okay?"

"Of course. Plan on having lunch with me. We can have something sent in."

"Since I'll be coming from the diner, I can bring lunch with me."

"Great. 'Bye for now." Ally went to the waiting room and invited the new patient in. She hid her surprise as the person entered her office and took a seat in the comfortable leather chair across from the desk. The name on the appointment book wasn't the name of the person sitting opposite her.

"Rachel, isn't it?" Ally said to break the ice.

"Yes. Rachel Arquette. I used a fictitious name because…because I don't want anyone to know I'm here."

"I understand. It's no problem. How can I help you?"

"I wanted to ask a question," Rachel explained. She compressed her lips and stared down at the carpet for a long minute.

Ally waited.

"Can a person…do you think a person can have sex with someone and not know it?"

Ally glanced at Rachel's very pregnant tummy.

"Are you unsure of the paternity of your child?" she asked kindly.

Rachel nodded, then shook her head. "I'm sure it's Colt's. I mean, this other guy's. But Den... someone else says it could be his. I don't remember having..." She looked at Ally in despair. "Surely I would recall *something,* if I'd had sex with another man. Besides, I was already...I realize now there were signs I was pregnant before—"

Ally waited without speaking while her patient sorted through her troubled thoughts.

"I'm not making much sense, am I?" Rachel finally said.

"I get the gist of it," Ally assured the nurse.

She questioned Rachel gently on why Dennis Reid—without mentioning the man by name—would claim the child could be his and found out Rachel had gone out for dinner with the doctor one night when they left the hospital at the same time. In her loneliness for Colt, who had left with no promises between them, she'd let Dennis persuade her to have a drink with him.

"I didn't know I was pregnant at the time," Rachel quickly explained.

Ally nodded. "Then what happened?"

"He insisted on giving me a ride home, saying I shouldn't be out walking so late, then he asked for a cup of coffee. So I invited him in. He was going out of town to visit family and wanted to make sure he didn't get sleepy on the trip."

"And then?"

"I'd gotten a bottle of brandy for Colt—I mean, for this other man—because he liked some after dinner. Dennis saw it and poured us each a snifter while the coffee perked. I didn't really want it. I could hardly keep my eyes open since I'd worked twelve-hour shifts all that week."

Ally waited while Rachel took a couple of deep breaths, then went on.

"We talked and drank the brandy. It seemed so innocent, and I'd been so lonely." She stopped, pain etched on her face.

Ally felt it with her.

"I don't know what happened next. I...I must have dozed off. I woke and realized the lights were out. I was on the sofa and someone was kissing me. I thought it was Colt."

Ally chalked up another mark against Dennis Reid. "Take your time and think it through. Envision where you were, what was happening, what you were feeling."

Rachel pressed her hands over her eyes. "I'm not sure.... No, wait. At some point, I realized it wasn't Colt who held me. It couldn't be. He was gone. Besides, he was always so gentle, and he whispered to me when we made love. This was someone else."

Rachel stared at Ally, her eyes going wide. Ally didn't say anything.

"We didn't...I'm positive we didn't make love. I started crying." She shook her head in confusion. "Dennis was very nice about it. He didn't get mad or anything. In fact, he acted as if I'd done him a

big favor. He was so...grateful. I don't understand.''

''Had he asked you for a date or otherwise expressed an interest in more than a professional way?''

''Well, he had joined me at the diner on a couple of occasions when we were eating there at the same time. I was usually waiting for Colt—'' Rachel stopped abruptly. ''Obviously you know I'm talking about Colt Rollins and Dr. Reid?''

''Yes, but whatever you tell me is confidential,'' Ally assured the worried young woman.

''Thank you. I sensed Dr. Reid was interested, but I was involved with Colt. I was in love with him,'' she confessed. ''I would never have taken another in his place.''

''Have you told Colt the baby is his?''

''No.'' Rachel blinked back tears. ''How could I? I wasn't sure. Why would Dennis lie about what happened?''

''Jealousy for a younger man?'' Ally suggested. ''Perhaps he saw Colt as a rival in both his personal and professional affairs.''

''Colt said Dennis had volunteered him for the New Mexico project without informing him until it was done.''

''Hmm.''

''He might have wanted to get Colt out of the way.''

Ally hid a smile as she let Rachel talk the situation through. The young nurse had a head on her

shoulders. She just needed to sort through the confusion created by Dr. Reid. The rat.

"Colt has won a great deal of respect from others in the medical community," Rachel continued, a note of pride for her love creeping into her voice. "Dennis was jealous about that." She paused. "Colt says he wants to marry me."

Ally smiled. "And you want to marry him. So what's the problem?"

Rachel looked woebegone. "It wouldn't be fair to accept his proposal. Especially since Dennis was intimating my baby could be his."

"Trust your instincts," Ally advised. "You're now sure it isn't."

"Yes. It's Colt's. But I don't want him to feel he has to marry me because of the child."

"That's your pride talking. What's your heart saying?" Ally asked quietly.

"Marry him at any cost."

"So?"

"What about Dennis? He keeps insinuating we were intimate. Colt has refused to discuss it. He says the baby is his and that's all that counts."

"Wouldn't a DNA test solve this whole question?" Ally asked, leading her patient to a conclusion.

"Oh. Of course."

"Why don't you tell Dr. Reid you plan on having one and ask him for a blood sample?"

Rachel's smile appeared. "Yes! I'm a nurse. Why didn't I think of that?"

"The same reason you were confused about Dr.

Reid's story. You're an honest person," Ally said dryly. "You may have been afraid he was telling the truth."

"I was." Rachel stood. "Thank you, Dr. McBride. I knew coming to you was the right thing to do. I *have* been afraid to face the future. In case what Dennis said was true. I couldn't bear the thought of betraying Colt and my love for him—"

Her voice broke and the tears came again.

Ally handed Rachel a box of tissues and let her cry out the worry and fears of the past nine months. When the sobs quieted, she encouraged Rachel to wash her face and put on fresh lipstick before leaving.

"And talk to Colt," she advised as Rachel left.

"I will. Right after I talk to Dennis Reid."

Ally smiled to herself at the thought of Dennis getting his comeuppance. The man was a troublemaker.

The twins woke for their afternoon feeding. Luckily, she'd scheduled time for it. She finished her last two counseling sessions, one with an older couple and one with a young couple who'd only been married two years. Both sets of partners were having problems that revolved around money.

While the twins slept, she worked on Gary's interest profile. He was a bright kid with an alert intelligence. He could go into any field that required great responsibility; an ability to concentrate and the ability to stick through difficult times. Medical research was one such field his interest tests indicated he would like. She would help him get the

necessary scholarships for medical school or whatever field he chose.

Driving home, she recalled Rachel's fierce pride, which had made her refuse Colt's offer to marry her for the baby's sake. Although that wasn't a totally bad reason if both were determined to make a go of it and raise the child to adulthood, Ally understood Rachel's feelings.

It was the same for her. Her pride had kept her from making a fool of herself when Spence had drawn back from her after their tryst in the moonlight. Pride had caused her to distance herself from him on the few occasions she saw him during their college years. It also made her wary of her feelings when he touched her now. That kiss at her house last Saturday after their guests left...

She drew a shaky breath. Four days and she could still feel it on her lips, could close her eyes and experience the pressure of his body against hers. Oh, God, it had been a mistake—to respond like that, to let herself yearn and want and need him. To let the hunger lead...

No, no, no. She was a mother now. She had duties to the twins. The children would fill her world. They would be enough to fill her life for years to come.

Spence balanced the plate of croissants filled with ham and pineapple chunks blended in cream cheese in one hand, laid a bag of chips on top and picked up the six-pack of beer with the other. There. He was ready.

He joined other singles from his building who were going to the Friday night get-together at the apartment complex clubhouse. His neighbor, Deb Cheassman, pronounced Chase-man, called to him.

"Hi, Spence, going to the clubhouse?"

He refrained from saying that should be obvious. "Right. Aren't you joining the fun?" he asked, noting her empty hands.

"Yes. I've already taken my stuff down. Here, let me help you." She took the platter and handed the chips back.

Spence saw a couple of guys glance his way when he and Deb walked in. Their glances were envious. She was one of the best-looking women in the complex. She worked as a researcher in the D.A.'s office, so she knew and understood his work. Another plus.

So why wasn't he attracted to her?

He grimly pushed the answer to the back of his mind, determined to enjoy the evening. It was time he mingled with his neighbors. And had some fun.

With the deaths of his father and brother, then the decision to move back to Buttonwood after his mom had asked him to consider it, the past year had been difficult. He still wasn't sure he'd done the right thing in returning. It seemed to have stirred up feelings better left unstirred.

"You're quiet," Deb said, leading the way to the tables set up along the side of the pleasant clubhouse. "Is this a natural trait, or is it some deep, dark secret that's weighing you down?"

He smiled at her teasing. "Nothing serious. I'm

thinking of bumping off a judge who's driving me crazy with his demands.'' He put the beer in a cooler of ice while she made room for the platter of sandwiches, then opened the chips and took one to nibble on.

''We plot things like that regularly in the D.A.'s office. I can pass on some tips I've heard if you need them.''

He laughed with her while she chose a soda. He twisted off the cap on a bottle of beer and glanced around.

''What's funny?'' one of the other bachelors asked, ambling over to them and helping himself to a beer.

''We're plotting dire deeds,'' Spence told him.

''There's Darlene,'' Deb said and waved to a blonde who hesitated at the door. ''Join us,'' she called.

Spence smiled at the new female. Her blond tresses contrasted with Deb's raven waves. Both women had blue eyes and were pretty and perky. The four became a group, settling at a nearby table and chatting easily about their lives. They helped themselves to the potluck selection and later danced to tunes on the CD player.

He realized sometime during the evening that he'd been set up. The two women had exchanged a conspiratorial glance when he'd mentioned he and Deb had happened to meet on their way over. He had assumed that Deb had forgotten something and returned home after taking her veggie platter to the clubhouse. Now he knew she'd gone home and

waited for him to come out of his apartment, which was above hers. She would have seen him coming down the steps.

Not that it mattered, he assured himself. He should be flattered that she was interested. He glanced at the clock on the wall. Midnight.

"Do you have a late date?" Deb asked while they danced to some old tune whose title he couldn't recall.

"No, why?"

"You keep looking at the clock." She gave him a flirty look from under her lashes. "Perhaps you're bored."

"You don't really believe that," he chided in a playful tone, knowing it was true. She was much too confident of her personal allure to think something like that. But the truth was—he was bored.

Inhaling Deb's perfume while he spun them around the clubhouse floor, he kept recalling Ally— the warm, healthy scent of her body while they'd worked together on assembling the crib and painting the bedroom. The way she smelled of baby shampoo and talc after bathing the twins.

He wondered if she was getting any sleep. He hadn't been over since last weekend. Not since he'd kissed her.

Deb snuggled up to him during the next song, which was slow and dreamy. He worried that the kids were crying and Ally wasn't getting any rest.

He felt fingers touch the back of his neck, then slide into his hair and make little stroking motions.

He recalled Ally's thick waves and the feel of silky tangles crushed in his hand.

Her lips had been pure ambrosia, soft but demanding, too, answering the passion with a hunger that matched his own. No surprise there. He'd known she was like that from those long-ago kisses they had shared.

Regret swept over him. He wished he'd done something differently that night. He wasn't sure what. It hadn't been the time to make love, not for either of them. They'd both had ambitions for the future. And maybe he'd been afraid of being tied down....

It was an insight into himself that he didn't like. He'd played the field during college, but he'd been fair. He hadn't made love with anyone. Not until after Ally and Jack were engaged. Then he'd become involved with a fellow law student for a semester. She'd accused him of being incapable of commitment. He hadn't known what she wanted from him.

He glanced at the woman in his arms. She smelled good. She looked great. She was interested.

But they weren't going to have a relationship. Until he got Ally out of his system, he wasn't going to become serious about any woman.

The question was, how did he do that?

The answer slipped into his consciousness as smoothly as butter melting on toast. He needed to make love to Ally.

Then would he be free of the need that drove

him to seek her out no matter what the consequences?

Maybe. He didn't know for sure. Logic had deserted him. There was only a stark need that haunted him....

Deb leaned her head back and smiled up at him, her gaze dark and soft the way a woman's got when she was aroused. He didn't know how to get the message across that what he was feeling wasn't induced by her.

After the dance, he told her he had an errand he had to do. Leaving her looking perplexed, then angry, he strode out of the clubhouse and went to his car. He drove the few miles to the other side of town.

There was a light on at Ally's house. Just as he'd suspected, she was up with the twins. He would stop and give her a hand, even if it was...twelve-thirty.

He cursed and drove on by. This was not the time to be visiting. Ally wouldn't like it. She was probably asleep, either in bed or on the sofa.

His body went rock-hard at the thought. He turned around in the middle of the road next to the city-limits sign and drove slowly by her place again. Hmm, there was another light on in the back. In the kitchen. Was she up with the babies?

He turned around and parked in the drive, then sat in the car, undecided whether to get out. He didn't see any activity in the house. Maybe Ally and the twins were sleeping soundly. Which was what he should be doing.

But first, since he was already out here, he would check, by looking in the window, to make sure they didn't need his help.

He crept out of the car, closing the door softly so as not to disturb anyone and sidled up to the window. Nope, just as he suspected—not a soul stirring. Ally had left a light on in case she had to get up.

Ignoring an odd sense of disappointment, he quietly headed back to his car. It was a damned fool's errand anyway and a stupid time to be out—

A police cruiser, lights flashing, hurtled down the road. He paused by the car to see what was going on. His heart nearly jumped out of his chest when it careened into Ally's drive and came to a sliding halt behind his car.

He recognized the sheriff. "Hank, what's up?" he called softly, stepping out from the shadows.

"Who's there?" Hank demanded, drawing his gun.

"Spence McBride. What are you doing here?"

"I got a call about a suspicious character cruising the neighborhood." He peered down the road toward Mrs. Snell's house, where all the windows were dark.

"Hmm, I haven't seen anyone," Spence told him. "But I just got here a few minutes ago."

"What are you doing in Ally's driveway at nearly one in the morning?"

Spence thought fast to come up with a plausible explanation. "Well, my mom's been worried about Ally. The twins aren't sleeping much at night, so

she isn't getting any rest. I, uh, was up, so I decided to see if she needed any help. However, the house is quiet, so the twins must be asleep.''

Another light clicked on in the house. Ally came into the kitchen and peered out the window. Spence waved. She opened the door.

"Spence? Is that you?"

"Yeah. And Hank Wright. We were just, uh…"

"Checking things out," Hank supplied.

"Oh." She sounded skeptical and a bit confused. "Would you like to come in? Rose brought a cinnamon coffee cake over earlier." She glanced over her shoulder as if in answer to a summons. "The twins are awake."

She disappeared from view, leaving the door ajar.

"Well," Spence said, trying to think of a reason to get rid of the lawman.

"I can't stay," Hank said. "I'm on duty tonight, filling in for one of the men whose kid was in an accident. I'll be off…since there apparently aren't any suspicious characters around."

"I'll keep an eye out," Spence promised.

"Thanks," Hank said in a curiously sardonic tone. He returned to his cruiser and headed back toward town.

Spence stood there for a couple more seconds, then went into the house. He got two formula pouches out of the fridge and placed them under running water to take the chill off, reflecting that baby bottles weren't bottles anymore, but simply forms to hold the plastic containers. Babies swallowed less air from the pouches, Ally had told him.

It struck him as odd that he found this fact more interesting than the invitation in Deb's eyes tonight while they danced. This preoccupation with Ally and the twins was disturbing, although he couldn't say how or why.

He heard Ally clicking her tongue, then speaking cheerfully to one of the babies as she came down the hall.

She entered the kitchen, pushing both bassinets in front of her. "It's much easier to take care of them this way," she told him. "I'm impressed that a bachelor thought of it."

"Yeah, right," he scoffed.

She cast him a swift glance of amusement. He dried off a pouch, stuck it in the holder and handed it to her.

She sniffed when he came close. "Have you been drinking?" Her mouth pruned up in obvious disapproval.

He thought of how kissing her would soften her lips. "A couple of beers earlier tonight. At the swinging singles get-together."

She didn't respond as she lifted Hannah into her arms. The baby latched on to the nipple and sucked vigorously.

"Careful," he said. "Your expression could sour milk at a hundred paces. Don't you approve of my bachelor life?"

"It's none of my concern."

"I danced with a pretty brunette tonight. I thought of inviting her up to admire my etchings."

"Why didn't you?"

Her tone was hard, her gaze a challenge. Hannah stopped sucking and stared at her mother.

"She isn't the one I want," he muttered.

Ally's cheeks took on a nice shade of pink. He had scored with that remark. Served her right for taunting him. And tormenting his nights. He was the one who wasn't getting enough sleep lately.

"Why were you skulking around the yard tonight?" she asked, changing the subject. "You must have scared Mrs. Snells. That's why she reported you to Hank."

"No, it was a suspicious character—"

He stopped as he recalled driving up and down the road…but no more than a couple of times…while he tried to determine if Ally needed his help.

"The nosy old biddy," he grumbled. "What was she doing up at midnight?"

Glancing at Ally, he saw her eyes were shining, although her mouth was stern. His annoyance gave way to resigned humor.

"Reporting me to the police," he answered his question. "I may as well be useful. You want me to feed Nick?"

She hesitated. "Please," she finally replied.

He lifted the boy into his arms. "Hey, fella, how's it going? You getting outvoted by the women in this household? Yeah, that's what I thought. It's okay. I'm on your side."

"What a hero," Ally mocked, but gently.

All at once, Spence felt better than he had in a week. He and Ally fed and burped and talked to

the little ones for the next hour. His eyes kept going to her, drawn like the proverbial pin to a magnet.

She wore no makeup, no perfume, no enticing clothes, but his blood rushed through his body as though she was sending come-on signals of the most blatant kind.

After they put the sleeping children to bed, they returned to the kitchen. "How about that coffee cake you mentioned?"

She hesitated, then nodded.

While she heated slices in the microwave and poured glasses of milk, he settled in a chair at the table and watched her. He was aroused, but peaceful. He tried to think of something to discuss, but his mind wasn't cooperating. It was on target with his body, his thoughts crowded with images of her and how she'd felt during that kiss....

"Your robe and gown are pretty," he finally said.

She flashed him a glance that held a warning.

"Is your personal attire off-limits?"

She brought the plates to the table, laid forks beside them and fetched the glasses of milk. She paused before taking her seat. "Yes."

The finality of her answer irked him. "Why?"

"Because."

"Because of that kiss," he supplied. "I still want you, more than ever."

"Sounds like a personal problem to me."

His eyes devoured her tousled hair, the sudden fire that she couldn't hide in her cool gaze, the

slight tremor in her hand as she tucked her hair behind her ear.

"You feel it, too," he said, unable to keep from taunting her as she taunted his nights.

She sat down abruptly. Picking up her fork, she regarded him with a stubborn tilt of her chin. "Not really."

He was tempted to prove she lied, but instead he ate the treat and contemplated the strange evening. "I had a miserable time at the singles get-together," he confessed when he finished eating.

Instead of asking why, she fled the table, taking the plates to the sink and washing them. Drying her hands, she faced him. "It's late. You'd better leave."

"You're nervous as a cat in strange territory. Why?"

"You know."

"Because of the kiss."

"Because of the passion," she said with blunt honesty. "It's almost two in the morning. I'm tired. So are you. Our defenses are weak, at best." She gave him a weary smile. "Let's not do anything we'll both regret."

"I don't think I would regret a damn thing." He strode across the kitchen.

She backed into the corner of the counter, her expression passive but her eyes wary. He stopped himself from following, from pressing for the passion he knew lurked beneath the surface of their conversation, argument, whatever.

"We have to be sensible," she told him. "This...this isn't the time."

"Will there ever be one?" His laugh was skeptical.

"No."

Hearing her utter the denial caused the hunger to surge anew. Along with it came the unreasonable anger that even he didn't understand. He shook his head as if trying to clear the murky pool of feelings she caused in him.

He stepped toward her. Leaning down, he murmured, "If nothing else has endured between us, this has."

Without laying a hand on her, he kissed her. Her lips trembled under his, revving up the desire to a roar. He kept his hands to himself, but lingered over the kiss, savoring it and the warmth of her mouth with his.

He heard her breath catch and quicken. His did the same. The flames soared between them. When she parted her lips, he stroked along their velvety surfaces, then delved deeply into the hot, passionate depths within.

The blood pounded unmercifully through him. He fought the need to explore further, to stroke her responsive body with his hands, his mouth, his body.

She made a sound in her throat, a tiny keening cry that pierced the web of hunger fast spinning out of control. He heard more than passion in the cry, more than surrender. He heard the sadness. It went

right to his heart and his conscience. He drew back, breathing hard.

"Someday I want to see you completely naked," he told her in a low growl, "and I'll look my fill, then we'll make love until neither of us can move. Then we'll know."

He headed for the door before his passion-driven side got the better of his concern for her.

"No, Spence, we won't," she called after him, stubborn to the end.

The challenge in her denial tugged at him. He paused at the door. "How are we going to stop it?"

He left then, putting distance between them. It was ten after two when he got home. All the apartments were dark and quiet. He lay awake until dawn.

Chapter Eight

The next morning Ally bent to retrieve the newspaper, which was partially hidden beneath a boxwood hedge, then straightened without picking it up. She couldn't believe her eyes. Someone had sprayed black paint all over the cottage. And it had only been painted three weeks ago when the carpentry work on the addition was finished. It was just the last straw.

The familiar rush of tears stung her nose and eyes. She was tired, she reminded herself. It had been almost dawn before she could sleep after the contretemps with Spence.

In addition, Nick was not sleeping well at all. She had finally moved him into her bedroom so his fussing wouldn't waken Hannah, who had slept six hours.

She sighed, no closer to figuring out her relationship, or even a neutral meeting ground, with Spence than she'd been at three that morning. Neither could she figure out why anyone would spray-paint her house in black looping lines and circles from one end to the other.

Nothing made sense anymore.

Staring at the house, she suppressed the need to sit down and cry over it all. There wasn't time.

The telephone was ringing when she returned to the kitchen after walking all around the house, surveying the damage. Not one wall had been spared.

"Good morning," her mom-in-law greeted her when she answered. "I thought I'd volunteer to come over this afternoon and let you rest or run errands or whatever. I want to play with my grandkids. Would that be okay?"

Ally was so overcome by this kindness that the tears formed again. Her throat closed up.

"Ally?"

"Yes, I...that would be great." Her voice had an embarrassing wobble. She swallowed hard, but couldn't get rid of the knot in her throat.

"Did Nick keep you up again last night?"

She managed to put a bit of humor in her tone. "Oh, yes. He is a very demanding young man."

"Just like his uncle," Rose assured her. "There were times when I wanted to give Spence back, but I couldn't find anyone to take him."

Ally laughed with the older woman, but her heart wasn't in it. A sigh worked its way out of her. "Someone painted graffiti all over the house last

night. I can't imagine who…or when. I was awake most of it.''

''So that's why you're upset.''

Rose sounded worried, and Ally was sorry she'd mentioned it.

''It was probably just some kids pulling a prank. I still have the original paint. It won't take long to paint over it. Since it's Saturday, I'll have all weekend.''

''Oh, honey, don't try to do it yourself. I'm sure Spence will be glad—''

''No!'' Ally regretted the sharpness in her tone. She tried again with a more reasonable inflection. ''There's no need to bother him. He's done enough.''

''He won't mind—''

''I'll take care of it,'' she said firmly.

''All right. I'll see you after lunch. I'm at the office, but expect to be home by noon. Shall I bring us something from the diner?''

''I have a pot roast on. Why don't you join me?''

Rose agreed to come for lunch, but only if she could bring dessert. After they hung up, Ally moved a load of wash to the dryer and added another to the washer. It seemed as if that's all she did in her spare moments. Babies sure used a lot of clothing.

She smiled. Things would get better. That's what Claire had counseled. She'd told patients the same thing. However, hearing it as a weary parent put a whole different spin on the platitude. She vowed never to use it again, even if it was the truth.

Shaking her head, she got on with her housework. Maybe it was time she had a housekeeper. She'd always liked taking care of her home herself. With only two of them, it hadn't taken much time, but now, well, things were different.

An hour later, she heard a knock on her back door. She laid the folded baby gown on the stack and went to the kitchen. "Gary, hello. What brings you out this way?"

The teenager's throat worked before he blurted out, "I heard about your house."

"Come in. We'll talk about it." When they were seated in the kitchen with a soda for him, a fresh cup of coffee for her, she asked, "What do you know about the paint?"

He looked miserable. "I know who did it. And why. It was because of me."

"Care to explain that?"

"I've been studying more lately. I've decided to go to college."

This last he said defiantly, as if she might dispute his right to so lofty an ambition. She nodded.

"Last night, I told Ram and Clyde I wasn't going with them on a...on a job."

He glanced at her to see if she understood the "job" was a robbery or something similar. She nodded again.

"They got mad because they needed a lookout for the night security at a warehouse. Ram told me this morning what they did to your place. They think you told me not to hang out with them. I told them that wasn't true. I got other things to do. But

they said I was cutting them out 'cause I thought I was better than them.''

"It's natural to be resentful when you see someone pulling back and going his own way. They're afraid you're going to succeed where they've failed."

Before they could discuss it further, Spence showed up, dressed as usual in shorts, sneakers and a T-shirt that proclaimed him a Prize Hog, a reminder of a fund-raising barbecue put on by the Shriners over the Fourth of July. Spence had helped by grilling racks of ribs for hours over charcoal for the hungry mob who'd attended the various civic events the city scheduled each year.

He checked the house, his face grim, then strode to the door when she opened it. The fresh mountain air rushed into the house, bringing the scent of wild honeysuckle. Spence took one look at Gary's guilty face and put two and two together.

"Looks like you need a paint job," he remarked upon joining them.

Ally poured him a cup of coffee. "We were discussing that very thing."

"I'll paint your house," Gary volunteered. "I'll get the paint, too."

"No need for that. There's plenty left over in the garage," Ally told him. "Do you have a couple of pals who can help? I'll pay standard wages for a good job."

Color rushed into the teenager's face. "I don't expect to get paid—"

"Why don't you ask Ram and Clyde if they'd

like to help?'' she continued. ''If they do a good job, I'll recommend them. Maybe they can start a business. Spence could advise them on setting up a corporation.''

''I'm not sure they'll want to do real work,'' Gary said, obviously doubtful of this plan. ''But I'll ask. They'll get paid?''

''I'll check on the going wage for apprentice painters,'' Spence told the boy.

After the teenager left, Spence turned to her, his gaze stern. ''Is this some kind of new therapy—pay the perp for his crime?''

''Gary didn't do it.'' She pushed a tendril of hair off her forehead. ''A couple of guys from his gang did because he wants to pull out. I think they need something legitimate to do. Could you help them set up a business?''

He didn't answer for a minute, then he gave a sardonic snort of laughter. ''How can I refuse when you look at me with such sweet appeal in those big blue eyes?''

Tension swept into the room like a tempest off the mountain. She tried to ignore it. ''Thanks.''

''I came over to finish the trim, then I'll paint the bathroom. Will that interfere with your plans?''

''Of course not. Your mom is coming over to stay with the twins at lunch. I'll be able to help—''

He cut her off. ''I'll be finished by then.''

She frowned as he walked out, going to the garage where he'd stored the paint and trim boards. She sighed and continued with the cleaning chores

and the laundry while the twins slept. When Rose arrived, the cottage was sparkling.

So were the additional rooms. Spence had finished the last of the work by noon, as promised.

"It looks wonderful," Rose commented after they toured the addition. "Spence, can you put up the curtain rods this afternoon? I think Ally is going to have to keep Hannah and Nick in separate rooms, with him being so fussy."

"Sure." He spoke to Ally. "I'll do it now, then get out of your way."

"Lunch is ready. It's only pot roast, but you're welcome to join us." She sounded stilted, which displeased her. She didn't know how to speak to Spence any more.

His smile was quick, showing pleasure. "Hey, don't knock it. Pot roast is one of my favorite things. I know how to make the best sandwiches with the leftovers—"

"Like that chopped-beef-and-horseradish concoction you came up with one time that burned everyone's tongue off?" his mother asked wryly.

Ally laughed, recalling the event from their teenage days. Spence had had the most ravenous appetite, easily eating as much as any other two people. His infamous sandwiches, which he'd learned to prepare as his after-school snack, had become well-known and were discussed throughout the county.

The three pondered the graffiti during the meal. Rose was worried about the teenagers being at the

cottage with only Ally there to keep an eye on them. "They don't sound very trustworthy."

"Gary is. I'm not sure about his friends," Ally admitted. "I'm hoping we can get them started on something constructive, something they can take pride in and where they can earn their money honestly."

"But that means work," Spence said. "They can make money quicker and easier by stealing. Their peers laugh at guys who work for chump change, as they call it."

"Someone has to try," Ally said, feeling stubborn about the situation.

"And that someone has to be you."

She bristled at his disapproval of her plan. "If you have a better idea, I'm listening."

He shrugged as if giving up arguing with her. "Where are the curtain rods you wanted put up?"

"I'll take care of the children while you two get the new rooms ready," Rose said.

Seeing the concern in Rose's eyes, Ally felt guilty for worrying the older woman. It was just that Spence could be very opinionated at times. He didn't trust her plan and made no bones about it. He could be right, but he might very well be wrong, too.

Besides, people needed a sense of pride in themselves and their accomplishments. Sometimes all it took was one person believing in another in order to change a life that was going wrong. She had to try to help Gary, and perhaps his friends, break the

cycle of their lives. In order for that to happen, someone had to believe in them.

"I really don't feel up to it," Ally protested.

"Nonsense," Rose said just as adamantly. "You've been cooped up in the house for months. It's time you went out and relaxed some. Besides, Spence is on his way."

Ally clenched her hand tightly around the telephone. It was rare that she got even the slightest bit irritated with her mother-in-law, but she was downright angry at present. Rose had set up a dinner date for her—no, not a date, it was a...a favor. With Spence. Without asking, Rose had made reservations at the country club for them.

It was just too absurd.

Now he was on his way to pick her up. Rose would be down from her house in a few minutes to baby-sit the twins. So it was all planned, and Rose wouldn't listen to her arguments about this being a bad idea.

"Put on that nice outfit I got you last year for your birthday. I don't believe you've worn it once."

Ally wondered if the tinge of hurt in Rose's voice was real. She hadn't worn the dress because she'd had nothing fancy to attend. A quiet dinner, even at the country club, didn't seem important enough.

"I've got another call coming in," Rose said, breaking into her thoughts. "Get dressed. Your reservation is at seven. I knew you wouldn't want to be out too late."

Rose hung up before Ally could think of a really

good reason to refuse. She went to her room and stood in the walk-in closet, staring absently at the clothes on the rack. It had been a long time since she'd worn anything festive. She took off the dress Rose wanted her to wear.

It was black silk with a fitted bodice and a layered chiffon skirt that whirled gracefully around the knees. The neck was high, but above the bodice and down the sleeves, the material was see-through.

Demure but sexy.

She slipped it off the hanger and went to change into black undies to wear under it. She was putting on makeup when she heard Rose enter the kitchen.

"I'm here," her mom-in-law called. "And here's Spence. He just drove up. Are you about ready?"

"Just about." Ally smoothed on lipstick, picked up her evening purse and found an evening shawl with silver threads woven into a swan design on the black material. She put on silver earrings and necklace.

When she entered the kitchen, Spence was there, chatting with his mom while they waited for her. Her heart went berserk, pounding out an erratic rhythm that disturbed her equilibrium. "I'm ready," she announced, sounding almost angry.

She regretted that surge of emotion as the other two turned toward her. Spence's expression was cool and remote as he looked her over. Rose beamed her usual smile.

"You look gorgeous. Isn't she beautiful in that dress, Spence?" she demanded of her son.

"I'd say the dress is beautiful because of her,"

he said, so formally it didn't sound like a compliment at all.

"Exactly," Rose agreed happily. "Run along now. I know when to feed the kids. And that they get a bath, then playtime before the feeding."

Spence held the door open. Ally walked to his car, aware of him following behind her. He looked strikingly handsome in a navy blazer and gray slacks. His tie was navy silk with a pattern of gold anchors and red hawsers. He was elegantly casual. He cranked up the engine and drove out onto the county road that led to town.

"Mom was right. That dress needed to be worn. You look good in it."

A much more sincere compliment than the one forced by Rose, Ally decided. "Rose is trying to push us together," she said, taking the bull by the horns, so to speak, and speaking her thoughts. "I don't know why."

His grin was sardonic. "She's been trying to marry me off for years. She's getting desperate."

"Thanks."

"Don't get prickly. I didn't mean to indicate you're the last resort. She thinks we're both wonderful people, and one wonderful person deserves another."

"She's very generous in her love," Ally said slowly.

"Yes. She wants everyone to be happy. Unfortunately, what constitutes happiness isn't the same for everyone."

Ally pulled her shawl closely around her, slightly

wounded that he obviously didn't see being with her as a happy occasion.

He glanced at her, his dark eyes seeing too much. "I didn't mean you, that I...that we couldn't be happy together..." He ran a hand through his raven hair, mussing its freshly combed smoothness. "Hell, I don't know what I mean. Forget it."

But she couldn't. Sometimes she thought she and Spence were in a Jekyll-and-Hyde situation.

During the morning, painting the bathroom together, they had fallen back into their teasing ways, laughing at each other's mistakes and mercilessly calling attention to the slightest defect. They'd worked together as if there hadn't been a break of many years between them.

But whenever passion reared its head, things immediately changed. The atmosphere became charged with hidden and not-so-hidden tension. Questions flowed between them, unspoken and unbidden.

Maybe it would be better to make love and get it over with. That would get the desire out of their systems. He was just a man. She was just a woman. Sex would be the same as with anyone else.

Except it would be Spence.

Her heart went crazy again. She forced herself to perform the deep breathing exercises she'd practiced with Taylor during Lamaze classes. The notion was insane. Insane!

"The shrimp are fresh," the waiter informed them once they were inside the country club and seated at a table for two by a window. "So is the

salmon. Tonight, it's grilled over mesquite and comes with a lemon sauce laced with capers and sun-dried cranberries." He explained the other specials of the evening, ending, "The chef recommends the salmon."

He left the menus and handed Spence the wine list.

"What are you going to have?" Spence asked.

"The salmon."

"Me, too. That will make the wine choice easy. They have a chardonnay that's excellent."

She watched the sun set beyond the western peaks. A sense of peace stole over the land as the heat of day gave way to the coolness of twilight. One more week and July would be gone, she mused. The twins would be a month old on August sixth.

Spence gave their order, then watched her for a few seconds before asking, "What are you thinking?"

"The twins are eighteen days old today. So brief a period, yet I hardly remember a time without them. They fill my life …" She trailed off, reluctant to share feelings that were mostly sentimental with him.

"I know. I feel the same."

Her eyes widened at this confession.

"Don't look so surprised. Men can have feelings for kids, too. Mom was right. They kind of grow on a person, even when they're screaming in your ear," he added with a quick grin, "or keeping you awake all night."

She smiled, too. Scenes from the nights when he walked the floor with her, carrying one fretful baby while she carried the other, formed and dissolved in her mind.

This was dangerous ground. The images were too intimate. They spoke of family, of husbands and wives working together to care for their young. She only allowed her thoughts to roam in this direction late at night, when she was tired and her defenses down.

When longing overcame common sense.

When the meal was served, cooked to perfection, Spence spoke of events in the town. "There seem to have been a lot of adoptions lately. Have you noticed?"

"Only my own," she admitted with rueful humor.

He chuckled.

It was a relaxed sound, and she felt her nerves unwinding. She sipped the cool white wine. It had been ages since she'd been out like this. She tried to remember the last time, but gave up.

"Mac Duncan adopted his wife's baby. Claire and Johnny adopted Lucy. Kyle Montgomery is adopting Emma's son. And you've taken the twins."

"True." She nodded and finished the glass of wine.

Spence filled her glass again, then his own. "Another interesting thing—that young intern, Colt Rollins, asked Johnny, right in a restaurant the other day, what papers he had to sign to admit paternity

and wanted to know if he needed a DNA test. Johnny was at the diner, waiting for Claire. He said you could have heard a pin drop for the next fifteen seconds.''

Ally choked on her wine. Recovering, she grinned so broadly she felt the pull as her cheeks bunched and her eyes crinkled in amusement.

"Sorry, I didn't mean to startle you," Spence said.

"That's okay. I'm just so happy for Rachel—"

"Wait, I remember that name. I heard her mentioned at the hospital the day the twins were born. Some nurses were speculating on who the father was. I remember it because they mentioned Mom's nemesis, Dennis Reid.''

"I'm glad it isn't him." To her horror, Ally heard herself giggle. She'd better go easy on the wine. She was beginning to feel light-headed.

"I'm relieved for her and the kid," Spence said dryly.

"I don't like him, either," she confessed.

Spence's eyes caught hers. She felt mesmerized by that dark gaze. She wondered if her pupils were wide, too, like his. Probably. Was it only because the lights were dim?

As a psychologist, she knew dilated pupils were one sign of sexual interest. She inhaled sharply and caught the scent of his aftershave. Another sign was increased body heat and the giving off of pheromones along the skin surfaces. Warmth spread in slow waves all over her.

"Would you like to dance?" he asked sometime

later when a group started playing in the adjoining room.

She thought about being in his arms. Tremors of hot desire poured through her. She shook her head.

"It must be after eight." She stared at her watch. "It's nine. I can't believe it."

"How time flies," he mocked gently.

"It *has* been fun," she said honestly. "I don't know how long it's been since I've been out like this."

"Don't," he said, his expression going stern.

"What?"

"Talk about you and Jack." His tone was a low growl of impatience. "I don't care what you two did. This is now. This is us. Nothing else comes into it."

She considered. "We're all composites of everything that's gone before in our lives." She leaned forward and gazed at him as worry rose in her. "Did someone hurt you, Spence? Is that why you've never married? Or do you never stay with one person long enough to form ties? Are you afraid of commitment?"

His face stilled. No emotion showed in his eyes. She regretted she had breached an unseen barrier between them.

"Are you analyzing me, Doctor? Don't. It's none of your business. I'm not your patient."

"I know, but…sometimes I worry about you."

His eyes locked with hers. They each searched for something in the other. She wasn't sure what.

At last he gave a snort of laughter. "Do you and

my mother consult on my love life, or lack of it, and try to decide what's wrong with me?''

While she thought about answering his sarcastic question, the waiter discreetly left the check.

Spence glanced at it, tossed some money on the tab and closed the black leather folder. ''Let's go. If you're ready.'' This last was spoken with only token politeness.

''Yes.'' She kept her shawl tightly around her as they made their way to the car.

The night wind was cool but pleasant. ''If we were friends, like we used to be,'' she said as he opened the door for her and she settled into the seat, ''this would be a perfect night to park beside the river and watch the moon rise.''

He slammed the door, then got in on his side. He drove out of the parking lot without saying a word.

She felt infinitely sad on the way home. She regretted the loss of her best friend. She was sorry for the passion that kept them from being friends once again. She sank down in the seat, weary, sleepy and morose.

''I can't help it,'' she murmured.

''What?'' he asked.

''The passion. I can't help what I feel.''

There was a long pause. ''Neither can I,'' he admitted in a harsh tone. ''Neither can I.''

''Time heals all wounds.'' Another platitude. She wished she hadn't voiced it.

''Ha.''

''I agree.'' She closed her eyes and rested for the remainder of the ride home.

* * *

"She's asleep," Rose said, entering the kitchen. "Poor darling, she was just beat. I knew taking care of two babies was too tiring."

"Huh," Spence said. He didn't feel so hot himself. However, he admitted his troubles stemmed from his libido, rather than the kids, keeping him awake.

His mom sat opposite him. She rubbed her temples with the fingertips of each hand.

"You've got a headache again?" he asked. This was another worry. His mother rarely was ill.

"Oh, it's not bad," she quickly said.

"Maybe you should have a checkup, see if anything's wrong," he suggested carefully. "Probably just need a vitamin or something."

"I'm fine." She glanced over at him. "You can go home. I'll stay and take care of the twins' early feeding so Ally can get some sleep."

He shrugged. "It isn't even nine-thirty. Maybe you should go home and take something for that headache. I can look after the kids tonight."

"You wouldn't mind?"

She sounded as if this would be a big favor. "Of course not. You run along. I'll be fine."

"I think I will. I appreciate this, son. I really do." She gave him a kiss on the cheek, picked up her purse and headed out to her car. In less than a minute she was gone.

Spence looked in on the twins, then kicked off his shoes and threw his jacket and tie over the chair before settling on the sofa to watch the ten o'clock news.

The anchorman came on and announced several tidbits for which there would be more news later. That was the last Spence heard before he drifted off.

Chapter Nine

Ally woke instantly from a sound sleep. She listened, but didn't hear anything unusual. The babies weren't crying. She fluffed up the pillow and tried to relax.

She'd been dreaming. That's what had woke her up. In the dream, a social worker had decided she wasn't a fit mother and was going to recommend the children be taken from her. Taylor had said she'd take them, but she'd let Ally visit them sometimes.

Ally knew the nightmare was an expression of her deepest fears. She loved the twins and couldn't imagine a life without them now. She listened to the monitors, but heard no noise from the nursery, where Hannah slept, or from the living room where

they had moved the other bassinet so Rose could take care of Nick while Ally slept.

She glanced at the bedside clock. Two a.m.

The kids were sleeping longer than usual. Feeling a need to check on them after the terrible dream, she threw off the sheet and hurried to the nursery.

Hannah was sleeping peacefully in the bassinet. Ally's heart melted, as it always did when she observed either of the sleeping children. They were so sweet and innocent.

Quietly, her bare feet making no sound, she sped down the hall to the living room. She leaned over the other bassinet. Her heart gave a giant lurch.

Nick was gone!

Hitting the wall switch, she flooded the room with light and had to wait a second while her eyes adjusted. She checked on the floor for the baby in case he'd somehow gotten out of the bed, then scanned the room.

She rushed into the kitchen and flipped on the light. Nothing. She clutched a chair as fear washed over her in a tidal wave, leaving her weak and nauseated.

"Nick," she called out as if he would hear and answer.

"What is it?" a male voice replied in a groggy tone.

Her heart thudded painfully. She rushed back to the living room and peered over the sofa at Spence. Nick snoozed peacefully on his uncle's chest.

Spence narrowed his eyes against the overhead light and glared at her. "Turn off the lights," he

requested in a low growl. "A guy can't sleep around here with all the racket. What's going on?"

She pressed a hand to her chest. "I thought Nick was gone. When I didn't find him in his bed, I thought—" She stopped abruptly as tears pushed to the surface.

Spence sat up, careful not to jog Nick. The baby stirred when he rose. "Shh, shh," he said soothingly. He put the baby in the bassinet and turned out the light. "Come on," he said to Ally.

She followed him into the kitchen. "What are you doing here? Where's Rose?"

He turned on the stove light and flicked off the bright overhead one. "I volunteered to baby-sit and sent her home. I was trying to let you sleep all night." He shot her a curious glance. "What's got you into a panic? Don't you think I can watch the kids by myself?"

"Of course. It was just…I had this dream, a nightmare, really. I thought someone had taken the children. When I found Nick's bed empty, I was frightened." She tried to laugh, but couldn't. "The dream was so real."

He nodded in understanding. "I'll make some cocoa. That's supposed to be good for the nerves. Meanwhile, you might go put on a robe or something. My resistance is only so-so at this hour of the night."

Ally glanced down. She wore nothing but underclothes. Black ones. Lacy ones. Sexy ones.

"Oh, Spence, I'm so sorry," she apologized, throwing her arms instinctively across her nearly

bare bosom. "I didn't realize...I mean, I was so worried..."

"Go," he ordered, a thread of wry amusement in the word. He took a menacing step toward her.

She fled.

Her hands shook while she slipped off the frankly alluring undies. Her skin was flushed. Yearning shot through her. She wanted...oh, heavens, she wanted so much!

None of it attainable. Hopes, dreams, wild longings, what did they matter in the grand scheme of things?

She reminded herself of everything she had—a career she loved, friends and family—no one could be kinder than Rose. Or Spence. And now she had the twins. Life was good.

Except she wanted even more—a great, all-consuming, glorious love. Someone to share all life's pleasures and sorrows. A soul mate.

She swallowed the painful longing that rose to her throat as the knowledge that her husband—through no fault of his own—hadn't been that person pushed its way into her consciousness. The restless sadness returned.

"I'm sorry," she whispered, knowing that was the one thing missing from her marriage. She'd given as much of herself as she could. So had Jack. But it hadn't been enough for either of them.

Going into the bathroom, she wondered if she'd ever find what her heart continually hoped for.

Spence wasn't it.

Part of her longed to rush to his arms and answer

the rampant passion she'd witnessed in his eyes a moment ago, but that wasn't the real answer.

He was caught in the desire. It would pass. And then? Then she would be left with more memories of them to haunt her dreams. To fall in love with Spence would be supremely foolish. She closed her eyes and willed her heart to obey.

Reentering the kitchen ten minutes later, her face washed and her hair combed, dressed in her ankle-length nightgown and matching robe, she felt much more composed.

Spence spared her one quick once-over, then poured the cocoa. He plunked a mug in front of her at the table and took the other with him to his seat.

"Did the twins have a night feeding yet?" she asked.

"Does the sun rise in the east?"

She smiled slightly. "You should have called me."

"That was the whole point of my being here—to let you sleep." He blew across the steaming surface of the cocoa, then took a sip. "Mom had a headache again." He looked worried. "I'm going to insist she have a checkup."

"She said she used to have migraines in adolescence. Sometimes they return at menopause." Ally thought about it. "No, she's past that already."

"Huh," he said.

He laced his fingers around the mug and stared into the whorls of steam as if preparing to read a fortune. A very moody gypsy, she surmised. There was an aura of unrest about him, as if his thoughts,

carefully concealed from her, were troubled and he resented that fact.

She studied him in a series of quick glances. He looked attractively disheveled. His white shirt was wrinkled from cradling Nick on his chest while they slept. His hair was tousled, reminding her of the way it had looked when they were kids.

A picture came to her—Spence racing her on their bikes, deliberately slowing down to let her keep up, his hair blowing across his forehead, his eyes full of fun....

Tenderness flooded her. He would make a good father someday. When he found the right person. When they got past the passion that arced between them like forked lightning. When he fell in love...

She took a gulp of cocoa and gasped aloud. Waving her hand in front of her mouth, she dashed for an ice cube from the freezer and plopped it into her mouth.

"Sorry. I got the cocoa too hot," he apologized.

"That's okay. You want an ice cube?"

When he nodded, she dropped one into his mug and one into hers. The silence settled around them, but there was an uneasy feel to it. The companionship they had once shared and had occasionally reexperienced of late was absent.

In its place was the hum of sexual tension. She was aware of the night and of him. For all practical purposes, they were alone in the house, two adults who wanted each other with an inexplicable hunger that wouldn't go away.

"The hunger," she murmured, giving voice to her thoughts, "it gets harder to control, doesn't it?"

He knew exactly what she was talking about. "Yes."

"What are we going to do?"

"Don't ask me," he said with more than a tad of irony in the words.

Silence.

"I know what I want to do."

His voice caressed her senses. He had a whisky-smooth baritone with a burr of western tang to it in spite of his years at school back east. Goose bumps rose on her arms.

She sighed shakily, willpower receding further and further from her grasp as longing surged.

"Ally—"

She couldn't resist the ragged need she heard as he said her name. She looked up and met his eyes. Common sense fought a brave battle with desire, but the outcome was predictable.

When he rose, she stood, too. He held out his hand. Fully knowing what she was doing, she laid her hand in his.

His chest rose as he dragged in a deep breath, then released it. With the gentlest of tugs, he pulled her to him.

The kiss was strangely gentle, not tentative, but patient, as if he was giving her a chance to change her mind at the last moment. She didn't.

His hands moved from her shoulders to her waist. They were large and warm on the curve of her hip. She stepped forward, automatically arching upward

until they touched along their chests and stomachs and thighs.

Fierce heat rushed over her, a forest fire out of control at the first spark. She had wanted him forever.

"I want you," she whispered when he lifted his mouth slightly from hers.

"It's mutual. You can tell that, can't you?"

"Yes."

He was hard and ready against her abdomen. She moved against him, aching for fulfillment, knowing they were embarking on a road whose end neither of them could see.

"I don't know if this is wise," she whispered. "I don't know what it means."

"Wisdom be damned," was his answer to her worry. "Don't think so much."

"If only life were that simple."

He paused. "Do you want to stop?"

She shook her head. "That's the only thing I'm sure of," she admitted, ruthlessly honest with herself and with him. Never could she say he had seduced her.

He released a heavy breath. "I feel the same. If there's hell to pay tomorrow, so be it."

"Yes."

His smile was solemn, his gaze lambent at her answer. He trailed kisses to her temple, down her ear to her neck. He left little bolts of fire to linger along her skin after he moved on. Her knees grew weak, and she clutched at his broad shoulders, needing his strength.

"Easy, love," he murmured, pressing kisses along her collar bone. "We have time, all the time in the world."

"Until the kids' next feeding," she corrected with a wry laugh.

She felt the laughter move through his body at her little joke. It felt good to joke with him again. Like old times. Like graduation night, when she'd been ready to give her heart, soul and body to him.

Tonight she would share her body, but no more. They would have this moment.

His hands moved to the front of her waist, then to the ties of her robe. He tugged and the bow fell apart. When he slid his hands inside to caress her back, she gasped as the blood pounded furiously through her.

"I don't want easy," she told him. "I want wild and frenzied and *now*."

He drew back. His eyes, dark as the night sky, raked over her face and delved into her eyes. "You mean that. You really mean it."

She smiled at him, no longer uncertain or hesitant. Whatever course they were set on, she was willing to see it through. "Tonight is ours," she said.

He nodded, and she knew he understood. They weren't fighting the need between them any longer. It was too strong. And it was much too late to stop.

Moving swiftly, he lifted her into his arms. She clung to his shoulders and nuzzled her nose against his neck. He entered her room and pushed the door

closed with his foot. Then he laid her on the bed and stepped back.

"I want to see you," he said.

"There's a night light on the lamp. The switch is on the bottom."

Spence felt a tenderness he'd rarely experienced. This was Ally, practical, independent, stubborn... willing...responsive...sure.

He turned the switch, and pastel light softened the shadows without completely eradicating them.

"You're beautiful," he whispered hoarsely. "So beautiful it makes me hurt, inside, in a place I can't describe."

"I know the place," she said, filled with the ache of anticipation. "I feel it there, too. The need, the hunger, they burn inside me, in that secret place."

Ally was intensely aware of him watching her as he tugged his shirt free, unbuttoned it and tossed it aside. His slacks quickly followed. His T-shirt and briefs were a blur of white against his tanned skin, then those, too, were gone. She feasted her eyes on him.

"Now you," he said, his voice dropping a register.

Spence sat beside her and pushed the gown up to her thighs. She lifted her hips. The gown flowed upward. The tips of his fingers stroked along her flesh as he removed the last barrier between them. The heat of her bare skin seared him to his soul.

He knew he would pay for this night...somehow, someday...but he was willing to take whatever the fates handed out as long as he had this one night.

He slid his hands over her, touching all the places the cloth had covered. The most wonderful pleasure he'd ever known shot through him as he ran his tongue over one perfect breast while caressing the other.

"Ambrosia," he said, saying things he had never said to a woman, needing her in a way he'd never needed another. He'd worry about that later, but not tonight.

Ally gasped in pleasure. Things happened to her, inside and out. Her nipples drew into tight beads. Heat flowed from him to her, her to him, from a magic place inside where passion bloomed. She writhed against him and ran her hands over his sides and along his back.

"Come to me," she invited, breathless with wonder. "This is so wonderful. Come to me now."

"Not yet. This has been too long coming to rush things. I'm going to make love to you for hours."

"I can't wait that long," she protested, but with laughter in her voice.

"I like that," he said, cupping her face in his hands.

"What?"

"Your laughter. It's been so long since I heard your laughter, when it was just for me, for the two of us." He brushed the backs of his knuckles over her breast. "And since we shared this."

"Years." Sadness filled her unexpectedly.

"Don't," he said. "I shouldn't have brought up the past. I don't want anything to come between us and this moment. I've wanted you too long."

"It's the same for me."

"Your honesty was something I missed. You were the only friend I trusted to be completely honest with me."

She clutched his forearms, her expression earnest. "Let's always be open with each other. If we have nothing else, let's have that between us. Promise."

"Promise," he repeated. He kissed her lips, then smoothed the curls from her forehead. "Ally, I didn't plan a seduction tonight. I never thought my luck would stretch this far. I'm not prepared...if we need...if you'd feel better if we used a condom, I can get—"

"There's no need. You know I can't have children."

"You're safe with me," he assured her. "I've always been careful."

She smiled at him. "I know that. Kiss me some more, Spence. The night seems to be rushing by."

"There'll be lots of kisses."

Spence touched her in all the ways he knew to give her pleasure. She was responsive—serious yet playful, full of fire and sometimes a sweet hesitation until she was sure he liked what she was doing.

"I love the feel of you," she murmured at one point, running her hands along his sides and down his thighs. "You can't begin to know how much."

"If it's a tenth of what I'm feeling, it's pretty overwhelming." He paused. "It's been there for years, a door we couldn't open—"

"Except for that one night," she reminded him.

"Yes. Magic and moonlight and just us. Like now." He fought for patience. He wanted the night to last. He wanted to thrust into her. He wanted fulfillment *right then*. He wanted to hold back until they were both satiated with the touch and feel of the other.

His heart reeled drunkenly, bouncing off his rib cage and generally being a nuisance. He shifted them so that she was on her back and he was on his side. Propped up on an elbow, he ran his free hand down her torso, then back to cup her breast.

"I'd wondered if my dreams of you were better than the reality. They weren't. You're still perfect," he told her.

"So are you."

Ally let him caress her for a while, then she pushed him on his back while she explored his body. She touched his chest, caressed his nipples until they contracted, then ran a finger around his belly button. She kissed all the places she touched. Then she drew a line down the center of his torso to his groin with one finger.

"I burn wherever you touch me. You always had the ability to set me on fire," Spence told her. He lifted a hand to her hair and caught a fistful of soft tangles. "I slept in that T-shirt for a week after graduation night. It had the scent of you on it."

It was the first time he'd ever confessed this to anyone. With her, he could be truthful.

She lifted her head and smiled at him. He saw the tenderness. And the sadness, which was tinged

with nostalgia and longings for things he couldn't decipher.

He found he wanted to erase those shadows. Like the fabled knight in shining armor, he wanted to make life perfect for this woman. His best friend.

She bent over him again. When she encircled him with her hand, he closed his eyes and fought for control. He felt a moist caress, then the smooth motion of her mouth on him.

He caught her face between his hands and brought her mouth to his. "I'll never last if you do that."

She pulled away, then sat up and studied him, her eyes wide and dark with passion. "I want to know all of you."

"Later," he said, the word a groan of need warring with control. He turned the tables on her, moving down her body until he could experience the full essence of her—the textures, the subtle scents of perfume and arousal, the honeyed moistness of all the hidden crevices.

Ally breathed deeply. She panted. She writhed and moaned as Spence worked his magic on her. "No, no, no," she finally gasped. "Now, Spence," she demanded. "I want you now. In me. Now!"

He came to her then, his body long and lean, wonderful in its blatant masculinity. He entered her in one smooth stroke. She trembled with pleasure.

"Oh, yes," she cried softly. "Oh, yes."

Spence felt the contractions in her body as she climaxed. It sent him over the edge. He plunged deeper and deeper into a great abyss of pleasure.

Ally had never experienced passion like this…like diving to the bottom of the ocean and surfacing in a new place, one of wonder and peace.

"The contentment," she murmured, planting lazy kisses on his neck as he rested, his breathing still harsh, against the pillow near her ear. "I'd expected the passion, but no one told me about the contentment. I'm all warm and throbbing inside…"

"It's the afterglow."

"Do you feel it, too?" she asked in wonder, finding this a wonderful facet of making love.

He lifted his head and gazed into her eyes, not saying anything for a second. In his eyes, she saw tenderness—a gentleness that was unexpected, a gift that came from the passion. Tears filled her eyes.

"Yes," he said softly. "Everything. I felt everything."

She sensed an air of resignation in him, almost of defeat. "Are you sorry for the passion?" she asked. "That we gave in to it?"

"It was the best I ever had," he assured her on a lighter note. "How can I be sorry for that?"

He shifted to the side, taking her with him so they remained joined together. She rested her leg over his hip and sighed, replete with the pleasure they'd shared.

She yawned.

"Don't go to sleep," he advised, nuzzling her ear. "We're not near through yet."

She feigned shock. "You mean there's more?"

"Hours. Hours and hours. I'm not letting you go until we're both drained and hung out to dry."

She laughed at his teasing. He kissed her again. His skillful hands moved over her, finding her most sensitive zones. To her surprise, she found she wanted him again almost at once.

"Oh!" she said.

His grin flashed briefly before he found her mouth once more. She felt him grow larger inside her, filling her with the pleasurable evidence of his desire.

Their hunger was slower this time. She found she liked that. They were more playful, less driven, although the passion was no less intense.

She pushed him onto his back and moved over him, taking her time, finding new pleasures this way. Later, he stood beside the bed, her on the edge of the mattress on her knees, as they explored different positions.

"I want to experience every facet of lovemaking with you," he said huskily. They were sitting in a chair, her astride his lap. "I'm greedy. I want it all now."

"I feel the same. I thought once would be enough, that then I would know...that *we* would know the passion and...and that it would be enough, just one time."

She was panting slightly. A sheen of moisture covered her body. His, too.

"It may never be enough," he said.

That was what scared her. She shook her head.

"It has to be." She clutched his shoulders. "Spence...oh...oh, help me. I'm going to..."

"Yes," he encouraged. "Push against me. Take all you want, all you need. I'm with you."

She experienced the shattering once again and held her breath as the world fell into crystalline fragments around her. She felt his climax immediately afterward as his body throbbed inside her. They returned to bed.

The aftermath was as before—a deep peace, like floating in a warm sea while resting in his arms.

She heard his breathing deepen as he relaxed beside her, his leg thrown over hers. She let herself drift....

She awoke at daybreak. Spence was nuzzling her cheek, his body warm and solid against hers. She looked at the clock. "The twins," she murmured.

"All snug and sleeping like hibernating bears. Come on," he urged. He led her into the bathroom and turned on the shower, then closed the door after them.

"This is new," she said, running her soapy hands over him, exploring his body more intimately, aware of his masculinity, the sharp breaths he drew when she touched a particularly sensitive place. "I've never bathed with another person in my life."

"You and—" he started, then stopped abruptly, looking chagrined with himself.

"No," she answered. "We were always busy, getting ready for work or to go out. There was never time for play."

He pulled her against him and kissed her hard. "I'm glad we got the chance to *play*." His expression became more serious. "I've often regretted that we didn't finish what we started graduation night."

"We were wise to stop. We didn't know I couldn't get pregnant. We had college ahead of us. It wasn't the time."

"And later, there was Jack."

She leaned her head back and let the water stream through her hair. "Yes. You two were always rivals in sports and grades, everything. Was last night part of that?"

His hands tightened around her waist. "Hardly. I outgrew the need to one-up my brother long ago. What happened between us, Ally, didn't involve anyone else, either in the present or from the past."

She sighed. "Do we have it out of our systems now?"

He looked slightly startled and somewhat grim. "What do you think?"

"I don't know. It's never been like that before." She paused as his expression softened and his eyes gleamed in obvious masculine pride.

He touched his forehead to hers. "That's what I thought, too. Forget the past. We've started down this road. I want to know where it leads."

"For you that might work. I have the twins to raise. I can't just indulge myself in passion whenever I get the urge. I have responsibilities and a reputation, both professional and personal, to uphold."

He turned the shower off, stepped out and tossed her a towel before dying off. "Do you think being with me will damage that?"

"It could." She wrapped the towel around her hair. "Although the adoption is a private one, Social Services could intervene if they thought I was setting a bad example. I won't have anything jeopardize my keeping the children."

He was silent while he secured the towel around his waist and found a razor in the medicine chest. "Mind if I use this?"

"Of course not. There's a new toothbrush in the drawer, too. Help yourself."

He shaved while she brushed her teeth, then he brushed his teeth while she blow-dried her hair.

"I wouldn't do anything to hurt you and the babies, Ally," he finally said.

"Oh, Spence, I know that."

She flung her arms around him, then quickly stepped back as their body heat combined and threatened to burst into a conflagration once more.

"It's just that the...the passion between us is stronger than I thought it would be. I've never experienced anything like we shared last night," she explained. And I don't know what to do with it."

He watched her, the odd moodiness back in his eyes. "We were once friends. I'd like to find that again, if possible. If not..." He shrugged. "But know this—I'm not going to disappear. Hannah and Nick mean a lot to me, and I intend to be a part of their lives. So if that means we cool it, I'll accept that. For now."

She was about to thank him for his understanding when a crash stopped her words. "What was that?"

"Glass breaking. Stay here. I'll check it out."

At that instant, crying came from one of the babies. Ally rushed into the bedroom and grabbed her robe. Spence dashed into the hall wearing only the towel, running silently toward the living room where Nick was.

She followed at his heels, jerking the robe on as she ran. She picked up the crying child while Spence examined the shattered glass.

"A rock," he said. "Someone threw a rock through the window." His eyes narrowed dangerously. "Your hoodlum friends again?"

"Not Gary," she said. "I'm sure it wasn't him."

Spence gave her a doubting glance, then went to the phone. "Get dressed. The cops will be here soon."

Chapter Ten

Hank Wright shifted the toothpick from one corner of his mouth to the other. "I'm sure it's part of a gang we've been having trouble with lately. I recognize the prints of their shoes."

"You do?" Ally had been impressed with the lawman during the investigation, which had taken up a good part of the morning. He was efficient and logical.

He grinned. "It doesn't take a lot to figure it out. They all wear the same type of high-top basketball shoes. That's part of their 'uniform.' Not very smart of them."

"I wonder if it was the gang Gary is trying to break away from." She was becoming increasingly worried about the teenager. Between his father tak-

ing out his frustrations on his son and the gang trying to stop him from leaving, his life wasn't getting any easier.

"Maybe Gary was the perp," Spence suggested.

She shook her head. "He wouldn't. He's too bright—a protective type, not destructive."

Hank glanced from her to Spence. She'd been aware of his quick, speculative glance when he'd first arrived three hours ago and found Spence there. Spence had explained about the rock coming through the window.

"You heard it? You were here?" Hank had asked.

"Yes. I stayed with the kids last night so Ally could get some rest," he'd replied without hesitation.

"That was real thoughtful," Hank had said without a trace of irony.

The twins had needed attention at that moment, thank goodness. It had given her an excuse for a graceful exit before the heat in her face gave her away. Both she and Spence had cared for the children while Hank and his team investigated the crime scene, as the lawmen called it.

Rose stopped by as the sheriff was preparing to leave. "I was on my way to church," she said, "and saw the patrol car here. Is anything wrong?"

Spence told her about the window.

"Do you think you should move up to my house for a while?" she asked Ally. "There's plenty of room for you and the twins."

"No—"

"Yes," Spence contradicted. "That's an excellent idea."

"It was an incident," Ally stated. "And most likely won't happen again."

"First it was paint, then a rock through the window," Hank pointed out, standing by the door. "It could be something more serious next time. I'll have my men patrol the area more often in the future, but that's no guarantee they'll be here if the gang shows up again."

"I'll stay over from now on," Spence told the lawman in a tone that boded ill for anyone he found on the property.

"I'll be fine," Ally stated quickly as Rose and Hank looked from her to Spence.

"I'll see to it," Spence said firmly, an implacable stubbornness in the set of his jaw.

She frowned at him. Hadn't she told him that very morning that she would not allow anything to jeopardize her keeping the twins? "I'm sure we're taking this too seriously." She turned to Hank. "I'll speak to Gary. If he knows anything, he'll tell me."

The sheriff nodded. "Keep me informed. Well, I'm off to another crime-fighting day in downtown Buttonwood." With an engaging grin, he left.

Rose stood. "I'd better run along, too. It's kind of you, Spence, to take an active interest in your niece and nephew's safety."

She touched her son's arm as she walked past him, a satisfied smile on her face. She stopped in front of Ally.

"Don't be too proud to accept our help. We love

you and the babies. We want to be part of your lives.'' Giving Ally a pat, she left the house.

Ally cast Spence a troubled glance when they were alone. "You can't stay here."

"Why not?"

She laced her hands around her cup. "You know," she murmured, unable to meet his eyes.

The silence became fraught with tension. She thought of the night just past. She didn't trust herself around him. The hunger was too strong. One night of bliss wasn't enough. She wanted more....

Her heartbeat went off-kilter. How many nights would it take to ease the need? No, she couldn't think about that.

"Yeah, we wouldn't want to let it become a habit," he said dryly.

She recoiled from the anger as he directed a harsh look at her. "It wouldn't be wise," she agreed.

"Thus speaks the psychologist." He headed for the door. "I have some things to check on. I'll send over a man to fix the window."

After he left, she busied herself around the house as a restless energy seized her. She stripped the bed and threw the sheets in the washer. Their mingled scent had lingered on the linens, recalling vivid impressions of the night—his exquisitely gentle touch, the intensity she had never thought to find in passion, the brilliant flare of completion...and the peaceful ending.

The afterglow.

She pressed her hands over her face. She would never forget. Never. Never. Never.

Dear God, she had to, or she'd go crazy with longing!

At four, while the window was being replaced, Ally received a call from the Social Services worker who handled Gary's case. "I have Gary at my office," she said. "His father is in jail. The boy has been beaten. His mother has asked that the boy be removed from the house. He and his father fight all the time."

Ally had a good idea how bad those fights could be. "Where are you sending him?"

"That's the problem. He's at juvenile hall. I hate to leave him there, but I can't find anyone who's willing to take him in. I was wondering if you had any ideas?"

Ally thought of Rose, but she knew the older woman would be uncomfortable with a stranger in her house. And Spence would come unglued. She couldn't think of anyone else.

"I don't have a spare room," she began regretfully. "No, wait, there is a place, a studio apartment over the stables that my aunt used to rent out. It's been empty for a long time. I can check it out and see if it's usable."

"That will do. I feel we have to get the boy away from his father. It's too dangerous for him. Either he'll be seriously injured or he'll commit murder."

Ally felt the weight of responsibility become heavier as she agreed to take Gary into her care.

She had her own children to think of. However, she couldn't abandon Gary to his fate, whatever it might be. "Can you bring him out?"

"The sheriff said he could send the boy in a patrol car. It will be about an hour."

When Ally hung up, she spoke to Hannah, who was on the table in the infant seat. "Well, we're to have company. I hope I don't regret it."

Hannah watched her solemnly. The baby was in one of three recognized wakefulness states, the one called "alert but quiet." It was one of the most important bonding periods between a child and its parents.

Ally leaned close so Hannah could see her easily. "Okay, what say we go check out the apartment?" she asked in a cheerful, higher tone than normal.

Hannah waved her arms in the air.

"Ah, you like that idea, huh?" She glanced toward the living room where Nick was stirring. "Your brother is ready for company, it appears. I'll get the stroller."

After strapping the twins in the double stroller, she went to the old stable, complete with dirt floor, that had been converted to a garage years ago.

She got the twins to the upper floor by going backwards up the stairs, keeping the stroller level as she tugged it up each step. She was panting by the time she reached the top.

"Your mom had better start a weight-lifting program," she informed them, "before you two get much bigger."

"I would think carrying them around would

count in that department,'' Spence said, appearing at the bottom of the steps and peering up at them.

Ally had an attack of acute shyness. ''Oh, Spence, it's you,'' she said inanely.

''Yeah. You expecting someone else?''

She pulled herself together. ''As a matter of fact, I am. The teenager I told you about, the one trying to break away from his gang, is coming to stay with me. I thought I would hire him to do the yard chores around here.''

A severe frown greeted this information as Spence climbed the stairs. ''Are you out of your mind? You're going to have a delinquent living on the place?''

''His father beats him up. It's too dangerous for him to stay at home.''

''What about the danger to you, not to mention Hannah and Nick, if his gang moves in with him?''

''They won't. I won't permit it.''

Spence ran a hand through his hair, the very picture of male disgust, at this piece of female logic. ''Like they'll listen? They could hurt you—''

''So could any nutcase who's driving down the road and decides he'll stop here.''

''That's a random event. This is a sure thing.''

''Actually, people, including gangs, are lazy. If it's too much trouble, they'll back off. There's no money to be made in hassling me. They'll find greener pastures.''

''Yeah, right.''

Before she could argue with him, she heard a car engine. ''Gary's here.''

She glanced around. Other than dust, the apartment was in good repair. She headed toward the stairs, pushing the stroller. Spence grabbed one end and helped her down.

Rose and the sheriff's patrol car arrived at the same time. "More trouble?" her mother-in-law asked anxiously.

"Not at all," Ally assured her. Then she turned to the boy getting out of the cruiser. "Hello, Gary. I'm so glad you're here. I've realized this past week that I need a lot more help since these two arrived." She nodded toward the babies who were taking in all the new activity in their serious way.

The teenager mumbled a greeting without looking at anyone. He pulled a duffel bag out of the cruiser and stood beside the vehicle in an awkward, ashamed stance. His left eye was black and his bottom lip was puffy. Ally could see another bruise on the boy's neck, partially hidden by the collar of his shirt. Her heart went out to him.

"Gary is going to help me out for a while in return for room and board," she said to the others as if this were a normal and mutually agreed-upon arrangement.

Rose immediately understood the situation. "How nice. I've been thinking you could use someone."

Spence was silent, but still frowning. Although he was taller and brawnier, he didn't look a lot older than the teenager. Spence wore jeans that were out at the knees and a T-shirt that had faded

to a hazy shade of green. A dark wing of hair tumbled over his forehead.

Ally remembered how she'd run her hands through the shiny waves in the wee hours of the morning. Only twelve or so hours, but it had been a time out of time, an interlude that seemed more dream than reality at present.

"Got everything, kid?" the deputy asked.

"Yeah. Thanks for the ride," Gary replied.

"No problem." The lawman said his farewells and left.

"Come on, Gary. Let's explore your quarters and see what we need to do. Everything has been under dustcovers for a long time. We'll need to check it out."

"I'll help," Rose volunteered.

Spence silently tagged along. At the steps, he took one end of the stroller. Gary took the other without being asked. Ally was pleased with his good manners.

Together the four of them got the large room shined and polished in no time. Ally parked the twins in the corner, out of the way of flying dust and cleaner spray, while she carefully rolled up old sheets that covered the sofa and matching chair. Spence checked out the electric wall furnace, water heater and stove. "All working," he reported.

Rose vacuumed the mattress, which was in good condition, and made the bed from sheets brought from Ally's house. The twins watched with interest, then went to sleep before the adults had finished.

Ally dusted, then arranged some plants she

brought from her home. She placed a planter of ivy on a table next to a window and set a philodendron on the counter in the kitchen area. "Once the windows are washed and I hang new curtains, this will look like a home."

She regretted her words when she saw tears spring into Gary's eyes. He busied himself inspecting the cabinets which still had a set of dishes, glasses and flatware.

"I'll bring you a microwave oven in case you want to fix some popcorn or something," Ally told the boy, "but you'll be taking your meals with me and the kids. It's just as easy to cook for one more. If that's okay with you?"

Gary kept his back to her and cleared his throat before answering "Sure." He arranged his meager belongings in the closet and the maple dresser.

Ally and Rose exchanged a glance that spoke of mutual sympathy for the youth. Ally wanted to pummel the father who had inflicted pain on his son. Watching as Spence and Gary carried the twins down the steps, careful not to jostle the sleeping babies, she experienced a painful tug at her heart.

They looked like a family, all working together to settle Gary in, the two males helping with the little ones. It touched something deep and personal inside her.

"Uh, my, uh, case worker said I would do the yard work and stuff," Gary mentioned as they crossed the lawn to the house. "Looks like the grass needs mowing."

"Come on, I'll show you where the lawn mower

and clippers are kept," Spence said. "Ally doesn't know how to keep tools sharpened. See how the grass is jagged and brown on the ends? The mower needs some work."

She smiled as the two men went in the side door of the stable where the former tack room now housed gardening equipment and a riding mower. Spence, true to his nature, was taking the boy under his wing.

"Gary needs a positive male role model," Rose murmured as she pushed the stroller into the house while Ally held the door. "Spence is perfect."

"Yes," Ally agreed.

Rose sighed. "He dotes on the twins already. Did you notice?"

Ally nodded, not trusting herself to speak.

"I wish…" Rose pushed the stroller into the living room and returned to the kitchen. "I wish he could find someone. He needs a wife and family of his own."

Ally felt a shock ripple all the way to her toes as she envisioned him with a wife and children. She realized she didn't want Spence to find someone. She wanted…

She didn't dare express the thought. It was too dangerous. "I'm sure he will," she said stoically and tried not to think of how that would change her life. She wanted him to be happy. She truly did.

"This is the most absurd thing I've ever seen," Ally declared, furious with Spence.

He ignored her as he went about completing the

setup of the tent, unrolling a mat and sleeping bag and arranging them inside.

"You can't stay here," she told him. "People will think…" She gave a huff of exasperation. "This is just insane, Spence. I don't need this!"

"Tough." He tossed the pillow onto his bed and zipped the bug screen closed.

"I'm going to call Rose," she threatened.

"Uh-huh," he said equably. "I spoke to her earlier. She thought it was a good idea to have someone here for a few days, a week or so, until we're sure things are okay."

"A week…a week or so," Ally sputtered. "You most certainly will not stay here a week!"

"Oh, I think I will." He started toward the house, across the newly mown lawn that Gary had finished only moments before. The boy was working on the side yard now.

Both males were obstinate, she'd found. Gary had insisted on starting his chores before dinner. Then the next thing she knew Spence was pitching a tent in her backyard.

"It's time for the kids' bath, isn't it?" Spence asked, entering the kitchen after kicking off his shoes at the door. Barefoot, he went into the living room and brought Nick back with him.

"Hey, fella," he said softly, "want a bath? It'll make you feel better. Hey, now, none of that," he scolded when Nick's face screwed up, ready to cry.

Ally retrieved Hannah, then ran warm water in plastic tubs in the double kitchen sink. "Okay," she said after testing the water with her elbow.

She undressed Hannah on one side while Spence undressed Nick to the right of the sink. They bathed the babies together, each of them keeping up a steady stream of chatter the whole time.

"Look," Spence said, giving her a nudge in the side. "Look at that. Now that's a real smile."

He looked ready to argue if she denied his claim. She took in the wide grin on Nick's face and felt that terrible achy, yearning dip in her heart again.

"He is smiling," she murmured, tears misting her eyes. "Oh, Spence, isn't that adorable?"

"Yeah," he agreed softly, grinning down at his nephew like a conspirator. "Yeah, fella, keep it up. That's the way into a woman's heart. Teeth or no teeth, you're gonna knock 'em dead with that smile."

Ally had to laugh. Spence gave her a wicked oblique glance. Her breath caught, and her heart danced around like a dervish. Her anger and dismay over the tent vanished.

"What smells so good?" he asked.

"I'm baking a chicken. I suppose you plan on staying for dinner?"

"If you have enough. Or I can go to the diner."

"Being agreeable isn't going to get me to change my mind about your staying here. I could call Hank and have you removed. I'm sure there's some law against unauthorized camping on private property."

Spence laid Nick on a towel and dried him off with much tickling and blowing raspberries on the baby's belly. Nick made gurgling sounds. Ally noticed how efficient Spence was becoming at han-

dling the children. Rose was right. He was a natural as a father.

A knot gathered in her throat. Although she played and chatted with Hannah, who grinned as much as her brother now, Ally couldn't dispel the sadness that collected in her like an ocean of tears.

When the children were dressed and ready for playtime, she went to the door and yelled to Gary that dinner would be ready in twenty minutes. He nodded, finished the strip he was mowing and headed toward the stable.

Since she'd cooked vegetables with the meat, she had only to make the salad, warm some rolls, set the table and put the food on a pretty platter. Gary knocked on the back door just as she got everything ready.

"Come in," she called, tossing the boy a smile as she placed the salads beside the plates and set bottled dressing on the table. "Sit on this side. Spence can sit over there and I'll take this end."

Spence had both babies in their bassinets in front of him and was taking turns playing patty-cake with them, using their feet to clap. Both babies were in the "alert wakefulness-active" state. It was a good time to start them on simple game-playing, which people did naturally.

Spence had good instincts.

That fact both pleased and saddened her. Which made no sense at all. Her emotions were topsy-turvy today. Making love hadn't solved anything. In fact, it had only increased her awareness of Spence a hundredfold on all fronts.

"Please help yourself," she invited. She took a roll and passed the basket to Gary. Spence cut off a drumstick, then paused. "What's your favorite part of the chicken?"

Gary looked surprised at the question. He gave a half shrug. "I guess it's all okay."

"Hmm, I like the thigh myself. You want this leg or would you rather have white meat?"

"Uh, the leg."

Ally knew, as sure as she was sitting there, that Gary had never been asked his preferences in food. Or anything else, most likely. It was a miracle he was a good, decent person. He'd had to fight for survival all his life.

She observed him as he watched and mimicked everything Spence did. When the twins grew fussy, Spence kept up a steady stream of chatter until the adults finished their meal.

"I think we'd better feed these two," he advised when Hannah puckered up and tried to get her whole fist in her mouth. "You want to lend a hand?" he asked Gary.

The boy's ears grew pink. "I guess."

"Great. Ally can do the dishes while we feed the kids. See? There was method to my madness."

Ally exchanged a glance with Spence as she got up to prepare the bottles. He was drawing the teen-ager in, making him feel part of the inner circle of the family. The way he'd done with her all those years ago when she'd been a scared and lonely eleven-year-old.

Her insides turned to mush. It was just that

Spence was so *good,* she explained to herself. How could a person keep from responding?

She acted as if it was no big deal that Gary was set to the task of feeding Hannah, who was more easygoing and sociable than Nick. She plopped the baby in his arms.

Without any helpful hints on her part, Gary held Hannah exactly the way Spence held Nick. He was a bit tentative in bringing the nipple to her mouth, but Hannah latched on and took over, sucking contentedly, her eyes on her caretaker's face the whole time she ate.

Once her initial hunger was satisfied, Hannah stopped nursing at one point and gave Gary a milky smile. Surprised, he smiled back, then ducked his head as if embarrassed to be seen grinning at the baby.

When Spence burped Nick, Gary did the same with Hannah, his movements somewhat jerky and unsure. Hannah didn't mind a bit. She loved having someone new to charm.

Ally hid her delight and finished washing up their few dishes and storing the leftovers. "We run an open kitchen here," she announced, "so come in and help yourself to iced tea, soda or food whenever you get hungry, okay?"

"Thanks," Spence said.

She rolled her eyes. "I was speaking to Gary. I've noticed you already help yourself without an invitation."

His grin was unrepentant. "Are we going to have

pancakes and sausage for breakfast? She makes the best ones ever,'' he said in an aside to Gary.

"Gary and I are. I don't know what you're going to have.'' She dried the dishes, then hung up the towel.

"Your mom has a hard heart,'' he told Nick, who stopped sucking and grinned. "Life is going to be tough, but don't worry. Your Uncle Spence will watch out for you.''

"Huh,'' she said. "He'd better not count on any help in that quarter.''

"You still going to have me evicted?''

"I should. Pitching a tent on the back lawn. Honestly. Mrs. Snells has probably called the FBI.'' She turned to Gary. "She's our neighbor across the road and down the way about a hundred yards. She reports us for anything she doesn't think is according to Hoyle.''

"Which is everything,'' Spence added.

"Especially suspicious characters.''

Gary looked from one to the other as she and Spence laughed. When her eyes locked with Spence's, the amusement faded. She was suddenly glad the teenager would be in residence. She needed a buffer between her passion and her common sense, which seemed to have taken a holiday the previous night.

From now on she'd be on guard. She knew how strong the attraction was. She would watch for the slightest hint of the hunger taking control and stamp it out.

Seeing that Hannah had fallen asleep, she took

the baby from Gary, laid her in the bassinet and wheeled it to the nursery. For a moment she stood in the dark room, recalling that it had been her aunt's sewing room, then her bedroom when she came to live there.

From its window, she could see up the rise to the next house, where Spence had lived. His bedroom had been on this side of the McBride house. They had sent each other messages by raising and lowering their blinds.

She rested her head against the window frame and watched the stars for a minute. She had loved having Spence for a friend....

Closing her eyes, she acknowledged the painful truth that dawned in her. She had loved Spence then.

She loved him now.

Chapter Eleven

Spence glanced up from the document he was reading when Johnny paused at his open door, then entered the office and sat on the corner of the credenza. He waited without speaking while Spence finished reading.

"What can I do for you, old man?" Spence asked, finishing and laying the paper aside.

Johnny Winterhawk wasn't a man for idle chitchat, as Spence well knew. In fact, until he'd up and married Claire, Spence would have said his partner was a loner. He was also a person of solid integrity and a champion of the underdog.

Johnny held up two tickets in his hand. "Claire talked me into buying four tickets to the high-school band benefit for Saturday night. It's a dance

and dinner on the grounds at the park. She thought you and Ally might like to join us. You both probably need a break from the kids by now.''

''Sounds like fun.''

''Good. We'll see you around six.'' Johnny tossed the tickets on Spence's desk.

''Uh, well, it might not be as simple as that,'' Spence hurried to explain. ''Ally is sort of not speaking to me.''

As in, not at all, actually, but there was no need to go into the intimate details.

A grin kicked up the corners of Johnny's mouth. ''Yeah?'' he said. ''I've heard rumors....''

Spence felt his ears heat up. ''Don't believe everything you hear.''

''Which part shouldn't I believe—the one about you camping out in Ally's backyard? Or the one where she's threatening to have you arrested for trespassing?''

''Both of those could have a germ of truth,'' he admitted reluctantly. Nothing like making a fool of yourself before God and the whole town.

''Hmm. What about the rumor in which you're madly in love with her but she won't agree to marriage? Or that you want to adopt the twins, which are, by the way, really yours, but no one knows it, including the mother.''

Spence was dumbfounded. He jumped to his feet. ''That's the stupidest thing I ever heard. Who's spreading that cock-and-bull story?''

''Pick either of the town's two main gossips and you'll get a good idea. Claire, being a female, wants

to know what's true and what isn't. Be prepared for some grilling on the subject Saturday night. I think that's why she bossed me into buying the tickets.'' He got up to leave.

Spence muttered an expletive that drew a smile from his partner. ''I suppose my mom has heard the rumors, too. She'll probably give me a grilling.''

Johnny paused at the door. ''I think she's the one who's starting them,'' he advised and ducked out before Spence could react.

Spence muttered more curses as he locked up and prepared to head out. Everyone in town had heard about his staying at Ally's place for three nights that week. On Wednesday, Gary had told him that he needn't worry, that he would watch out for the doc and the twins.

Spence had realized the kid was as much under Ally's spell as every male who came into her orbit. He'd also realized he was being damned stupid— sleeping on the hard ground when he had a perfectly good bed at his condo. So he'd turned tail and crept back home in the wee hours yesterday morning, leaving Ally with her moonstruck protector and the equally smitten sheriff.

So be it. He wasn't going to worry about her.

He paused on his way out. Ally thought she understood human nature, but she judged others by her own values. Not everyone measured up. He'd tried to explain that to her, but she had just looked at him without any expression until he'd finished his little soliloquy.

Well, he'd done his best. She was on her own from now on. Far be it from him to butt into her life.

He locked the side door and drove home. After changing into shorts and a ragged T-shirt, he twisted the cap off a beer and moseyed out onto the patio.

His neighbor, also in shorts, but with a red halter top, came into view on the lawn below him. "Hi," she called up, her eyes alert with interest, her smile inviting.

It was nice to be appreciated, especially by a gorgeous woman. "Hi, yourself." He held up the beer. "Join me?"

She nodded and climbed the steps. He fetched a brew for her. They settled into padded patio chairs.

"Hard day at the office?" she asked.

"Hard week," he corrected.

"Too bad."

Her voice was a croon of sympathy. He forced himself to relax. "Ah, this is the life," he said, making a sweeping gesture toward the nearby golf green and the pond beside it.

"You haven't been around much lately," she said, her voice sultry with promise. "I was wondering if you liked living here."

"Sure."

He wondered if he did. More than once of late, he'd thought about getting a house, having a few acres to putter around in. He'd been raised on the outskirts of town and was used to more privacy.

Living in a condo was akin to living in the proverbial fishbowl.

"You left the pot-luck supper early."

The reminder irritated him. Didn't women know
that, unless a man had committed himself to her,
whether as a lover or merely as a date, she had no
right to criticize how he spent his time or track his
comings and goings?

"I thought of something I needed to check."

"Oh?"

She was fishing for information. Another irritat-
ing point. Why didn't she just ask what she wanted
to know?

Huh. She'd probably heard the absurd rumors
about him and Ally and the twins. And she wanted
to know if he was committed elsewhere.

Was he?

The idea hit him squarely between the eyes. No,
of course he wasn't. Him and Ally? Ha! They
hadn't been friends in years.

But they'd been lovers...for one night.

Heat swept into him like a grass fire fed by gale-
force winds. That night had been the most exciting
and the most satisfying he'd ever spent with a
woman.

He studied his pretty neighbor. She'd been flirt-
ing with him ever since he'd moved in. He was
flattered, but...nothing was going to come of it. Not
until things were resolved between him and Ally.
"Well," he said, "I have some work to do, legal
briefs and all."

Her eyes frosting over, she took the hint and left.

He figured that would be the last he saw of her. It didn't bother him a bit. He worried about the lack of emotion he felt at dismissing a pretty female. He was probably insane....

''There's extra formula made up. It's in the refrigerator. You have my cell-phone number? It's written on the phone book, right here on the front cover. Call if you need me.''

Rose patted Ally's shoulder. ''We'll be fine.'' She glanced over her shoulder. ''Won't we?''

Gary nodded, his shy smile appearing briefly. He was holding Hannah and playing patty-cake with her the way he'd seen Spence do earlier that week. Nick was on a quilt on the floor, making swimming motions with his arms and legs. He gave her a grin when he heard her voice.

Ally glanced worriedly from one to the other. ''It's so odd,'' she murmured. ''Twenty-five days ago, I was scared to death I'd never to able to manage twins. Now I'm worried about leaving them for a few hours because no one else can possibly know what they need when they cry.''

''That's known as motherhood,'' Rose assured her.

Ally smiled at her mother-in-law and impulsively gave her a hug. ''I really appreciate your baby-sitting for me.''

''You know I love it,'' Rose said. ''With Gary here for reinforcement, we'll be fine.''

''Okay, I'm off,'' Ally said with more confidence

than she felt. Actually, she was tired. A solid night's sleep appealed to her more than a night out.

She'd been rather lethargic all week. Not only that, but her feet had been swollen by the time she got home in the evening after her four-hour stint at the office. Taylor had commented yesterday at lunch that Ally's eyes looked puffy. Maybe she was coming down with something.

Fishing her keys out of her purse, she headed for the car. And a fun night out, she thought mockingly as she made the ten-minute trip to the park. She did look forward to seeing Claire and Johnny. She wasn't so sure about Spence.

He'd been gone Wednesday morning when she got up for the kids' first feeding. He'd taken down his tent and left without a word. That had made her angry. But she'd also been angry with him for staying.

Well, the whole situation had been ridiculous. He'd made her the laughingstock of the town. She'd told him so on Tuesday night...after Taylor's visit, during which she had recounted all the stupid rumors flying around about them and the twins.

"Honestly," she muttered in disgust as she pulled into a parking space behind a black pickup. She climbed out of her compact auto and glanced around the park where the locals had gathered for the fun and to raise money for new uniforms for the high-school marching band.

"Over here," Claire called.

Ally spotted them. Her eyes met Spence's dark gaze as she approached the other three. She smiled

and nodded as if they were distant acquaintances. She and Claire hugged, then she gave Johnny an air kiss near his cheek.

"How are the twins?" Claire asked, an unnecessary question since she'd just seen them in her office two days ago for a checkup. "Are they sleeping better?"

"Hannah is a dream. Nick is a nightmare," Ally replied with a laugh.

"Hey," Spence protested. "That's malicious slander. Nick and I might have to pursue this if you keep talking that way."

He moved the picnic bench out so she could easily slide in, then scooted it back into place and took a seat beside her. She was instantly aware of him all along her side.

"He cried most of last night, then promptly went to sleep when the sun came up. Rose and Gary are determined to keep him awake until I get home so he'll sleep the rest of the night."

"Sounds like a plan," Claire approved.

"Is Lucy still growing like a weed?"

Johnny laughed. "And then some. I never knew gals could pig out as much as guys."

Claire elbowed him. "Ladies do not pig out. Speaking of which, I'm starved. When do we get to eat?"

Ally laughed at their teasing. Beside her, she heard Spence's deep chuckle and glanced his way.

He wore a blue chambray work shirt, the sleeves rolled back on his forearms. His black felt cowboy hat was set at a slight angle, giving him a daring,

rakish air. His jeans fit his long, lanky frame like a second skin. She swallowed and looked away.

The mayor began a speech of thanks for the good turnout for the fund-raiser and pointed out how important activities such as the band could be for students.

Ally only half listened. She was worried about being there. She shouldn't have let Rose and Claire badger her into coming tonight. It was too much. Her emotions were in turmoil. She was by turns giddy, depressed, light-headed and down in the dumps. Nothing made sense any more.

Except she did love Spence.

She'd had to face that fact and live with it. Spence. Her childhood friend. Her lover of one night. Her beloved.

"Heavy thoughts?"

She gazed into his eyes at the question and saw concern within those fathomless depths. She shook her head. "Just a little tired."

"You're losing weight," he remarked, applauding with the crowd when the mayor finished.

"I seem to eat on the run these days."

His face hardened. "I thought I'd come over and set up the other bed and get the furniture moved into the new bedrooms. Mom said the twins could move in now that the paint is dry and the rooms aired out."

"That would be kind."

Anger flashed in his eyes, then disappeared into the darkness of his hidden emotions. "That's me," he mocked, "too kind for words."

"Are you two quarreling?" Claire demanded while Johnny observed them in his quiet way.

"No," she said.

"Maybe," Spence contradicted.

She refused to dignify that remark by responding. Instead she watched while a combo of high-school seniors assembled to play for the dancing part of the festivities. The mayor informed them the other band members would serve them shortly.

Soon they were eating barbecued chicken, corn on the cob, slaw and baked beans. Baskets of rolls were set on each table, along with butter and salt and pepper.

"Watermelon slices are on the table next to the grill when you're ready for dessert," the mayor advised.

In a few minutes, several teenagers went to the dance floor. Other couples followed as they finished the meal.

Ally swung a foot in time to the music and remembered going to her first school dance. She'd been alone and nervous. Spence had spotted her and left the girl he'd been dating all semester. He'd made the dance fun for Ally, bringing her into the circle of his friends and, she felt sure, somehow ensuring she danced with several guys.

Her hero.

A soft smile stole into her heart. If he wanted to be lovers for a while, until he got over his mad passion for her, she wasn't going to fight it any longer. When it was over, then she would work on being friends with him again, not just for the twins'

sake, but for her own. She wanted her long-lost friend back.

"Look," Claire said. "There's Rachel Arquette. And Colt Rollins."

"And Dennis Reid," Johnny added, an ominous note in his deep voice as he nodded toward the older man who stood at the back of the crowd.

A chill crept through the warm evening air. Ally sensed trouble brewing. Rachel had been the subject of a fair share of gossip, too. Ally knew how that felt now. If anything happened tonight, she would go to Rachel as a friend. She figured the young woman would need all the help she could get, the way Dr. Reid was glaring at her and Colt.

"Trouble," Spence murmured. He leaned toward her. "Stay out of the way. Johnny and I will handle it."

"There's the sheriff," Claire told them. "He'll take care of Dennis Reid if he tries anything."

Ally realized Claire knew about Rachel's problems and was on the young nurse's side as well. She relaxed. All would work out....

When Johnny escorted Claire to the dance pavilion, Spence hesitated a second. He was pretty sure Ally didn't want to dance with him.

What gave you the first clue? some ruthless part of him prodded cynically.

The fact that she had hardly looked his way for over an hour? The fact that she had hardly spoken to him unless he forced it with a direct question?

He shifted restlessly on the hard bench. He was

aware of turmoil inside him, in that deep, hidden place he'd mentioned to Ally the night they'd made love. He didn't like riling that place. It hurt.

The hell of it was, he couldn't say why.

"Come on," he muttered. His tone was not conducive to persuading a female to dance with him.

Obviously startled, Ally stood when he did. He took her arm and escorted her to the dance floor, feeling more like a warden with a prisoner than a man with a date. Not that this evening was a date. It was more on the order of enemies meeting during an enforced truce.

He heaved a deep breath as he turned and held out his arms. She stepped forward and laid one hand in his, the other on his shoulder. There was a respectable six inches between them.

Anger surged in him. On an impulse, he hauled her close so that they touched on all fronts. He knew at once he'd made a serious tactical error.

Hunger ran rampant through him. Ally stiffened at the intimate contact, but there wasn't a damn thing he could do to disguise the rigid evidence of his desire.

"Sorry," he murmured close to her ear. "Can't be helped. One night wasn't enough."

She surprised him by relaxing, then looking up at him. His heart did funny things when she smiled.

"I know," she said and sighed.

Her manner was sad, resigned, perhaps touched with irony. He welcomed the graceful curve of her body as she relaxed against him. Something wild

and impetuous and wholly masculine trumpeted through him.

"Are you going to quit fighting me?" he asked, curious about her state of mind.

"I don't know," she admitted in her honest way. "I think it's myself I've been fighting."

Another couple danced by them, the woman's shoulder brushing Ally's. Spence moved away.

"Dr. McBride," the woman said. "How are you?"

Spence realized he'd rarely heard Ally spoken to in her professional mode. Pride rushed in, adding to the confusion of the other emotions she engendered in him.

"I'm fine. It's a lovely night for the dance, isn't it?" Ally responded. "Spence, have you met Rachel Arquette? She's a nurse at the clinic."

After they spoke, the pretty nurse introduced her dance partner. "This is Colt Rollins. Dr. Rollins."

"Colt," he said firmly.

"Spence McBride," Spence said, noticing the nurse's cheeks redden as she introduced her date. He also noted the woman was very pregnant. Like nine months and counting.

"You're Johnny Winterhawk's partner, aren't you?" the young doctor inquired.

"Yes."

Spence thought the man would have said more, but the nurse sent him such a pleading glance that even Spence realized she was asking him not to pursue the topic. Yeah, looked like there was a pa-

ternity case in the offing, only this time it was the father demanding to be acknowledged.

Humans. What a crazy bunch.

He brought Ally closer as the couple moved off and rested his cheek on her temple. They moved together perfectly. They should. They'd learned to dance in his kitchen, his mom and dad showing them the steps while Jack had jeered at his efforts.

The dance ended, and he reluctantly had to let her go. Another guy, a doctor who had an office in the same building as Ally, came over and asked her to dance. She went with the man to the floor.

"When are you going to tell Ally how you feel?" Claire inquired, stopping beside him.

Distracted, he frowned at his partner's wife. Johnny had been detained by the mayor, who was expounding on some subject and gesturing energetically.

"About what?" he asked, trying for a polite tone.

Claire grinned. "I think you know." Her face became serious as she glanced at Ally and the doctor. "Life becomes much easier if both parties are open about a relationship."

"What relationship?"

"Ah-ha," she said and shook her head.

Her eyes were filled with laughter. Spence couldn't figure out what she found so amusing.

"I think you're in for an awakening," she added mysteriously. "And so is Ally."

Claire glanced over her shoulder. Spence saw her expression change to one of alarm. At that moment, he heard a female's voice raised in protest.

"Don't! Oh, please, stop, both of you!"

Spence took in the situation at a glance. Dennis Reid yanked Rachel Arquette out of the younger doctor's arms. The nurse was between the men, pleading with them. Ally left the doctor in the middle of the dance and started for the other couple.

Spence muttered a curse and headed across the pavilion floor. From the corner of his eye, he saw Johnny moving in, too. As in their days of playing football, he covered one side of the field while Johnny took the other, each ready to catch the pass or act as offensive blocks, whatever was called for.

Before they could reach the other couple, though, Dennis Reid gave Colt Rollins a shove that set the younger doctor back on his heels. Colt reacted at once. Taking one step forward, then shifting to his left foot, he let fly a right uppercut with the full force of his weight behind it.

Reid's head snapped back. Spence couldn't suppress a smile as the man's legs buckled. Then Reid righted himself and waded in, rage in his eyes as he lunged for Rollins.

"Stop them," he heard Claire say behind him.

"I intend to," he assured her. Before Ally caught a fist in the eye. She had almost reached the fighting men.

Spence broke into a run, darting around or between couples. Claire was right behind him. Johnny did the same from the other side. The sheriff, out of uniform and holding a soda can, was hot on his heels while the mayor lingered safely out of harm's way.

"Hold it, you two," Hank ordered.

As the struggling men paused, Ally and the very pregnant nurse stepped between them. Spence gritted his teeth.

Rachel pressed a tissue to Rollins's bleeding nose. Spence moved Ally out of the way and took hold of Reid's arm. The chief of staff tried to shake him off and get at Rollins again. He cursed at the other doctor.

Johnny grabbed Colt by his arms as the younger man put Rachel behind him and started forward.

"None of that, or I'll have to haul you both in," Hank told them. He gave each man a disgusted look. "My only day off this week and I have to waste it on you two."

"Tell him to keep away from Rachel," Colt told the sheriff. "That's my baby she's carrying—"

"You real sure of that?" Reid sneered.

Rachel put both hands over her face. Ally and Claire stepped protectively to her side and wrapped their arms around the younger woman. Johnny tightened his grip on Colt as the young man struggled to get free.

"Get this through your thick head," Colt growled. "Rachel is going to marry me. Me and no one else!"

Spence found he wanted to sock Reid, too, as the man pushed out his chin arrogantly. "After you abandoned her, she came to me. She needed my help."

"You creep," Colt snarled, fighting Johnny's hold. "I never deserted her. You sent me away so

you could move in. But she's mine.'' He glanced around the staring crowd. ''And now you and the whole town know it. So will she as soon as I can get her alone.'' His face softened as he looked at the nurse. ''Rachel,'' he said.

Spence felt a distinct kindred with Rollins. He knew how it felt to want a woman to the exclusion of anyone else. He wanted Ally that way.

''Marry me,'' Colt said in a softer tone.

''You're fired,'' Dennis Reid informed his rival. ''You'll get no recommendation from the clinic.''

Spence smiled. ''You can't fire anyone without the executive administrator's approval.''

''And you can't withhold a recommendation for personal reasons. I believe we can collect affidavits from doctors Rollins has worked with,'' Johnny put in.

Reid glared from one to the other. Finally his eyes settled on Hank Wright. ''I want this man arrested for assault.''

Hank shook his head. ''You shoved him first. Saw you myself. That makes it self-defense.''

Spence saw the quick smile that Ally tried to hide. Claire didn't bother. She grinned openly at Johnny.

''You two get out of here and settle your problems,'' Hank told the young lovers. He frowned sternly at the chief of staff. ''You better go home and take care of that eye, Doc. A frozen sack of peas works good for me.''

Spence released Reid, who stalked off after a

glare at everyone in sight. Johnny let go of Colt's arms.

The young doctor went to Rachel and slipped an arm around her waist. "I mean it, Rach. You have to marry me."

"Because of the baby?" Ally asked.

Spence was surprised at the question. It was obvious the guy was crazy about Rachel.

Colt gave Ally a frown. "Because I love her. I have ever since we met."

"Oh, Colt," Rachel said. "Do you really?"

"Well, of course. Why else was I working my butt off trying to get back here as fast as possible? You had me worried. You didn't answer the messages I left at the hospital."

"I didn't get them."

Colt muttered an imprecation. The couple walked off arm in arm, both talking at once about the past few months and the trials they'd been through. Spence heard the doctor repeat his proposal of marriage. Rachel accepted. Several people around them, hearing her, cheered.

"Has anyone said 'all's well that ends well'?" Claire asked.

Spence laughed with Johnny and Ally, her husky laughter flowing into him like some soothing balm.

"I think we ought to get married, too," he said, the thought coming to him out of the blue. "It's the perfect solution. In fact, it's the *only* solution."

Why hadn't he thought of it before?

She turned to him, her mouth open in surprise. He grinned as her eyes filled with wonder and a

sweet, radiant glow that reminded him of the way she'd looked after their lovemaking.

"Why?" she asked.

"It's best," he assured her in his most reasonable tone. "You need me to take care of you and the kids."

The wonder left her eyes. Fury settled in. "I wouldn't marry you if you came wrapped in gold and were the last eligible bachelor in Buttonwood!"

Chapter Twelve

"She's not speaking to me," Spence explained.

Johnny nodded sympathetically. "Life is hard."

"Doesn't make sense, does it? I ask her to marry me and she flies off the handle. Refuses a perfectly honorable proposal right in front of everyone. But did I get mad?"

"Not a bit." Johnny grinned and took a swig of his favorite Kentucky bourbon.

They were at a bar down the street from the office. It was a gathering place for the legal eagles in the community, just as the diner was for the medical people.

Spence had stopped in to discuss a settlement with another attorney that both their clients should be happy with. Then he'd stayed and had another

drink. He'd been alone until his partner had showed up.

"I was the reasonable one," he continued, nodding at Johnny's agreement.

"Right."

"What are you grinning about?"

"I've never seen you polluted before."

"Oh," Spence said. He felt an explanation was called for. "I got drunk once in college. Made me sick as a dog. I decided that wasn't fun at all."

"A wise decision."

"Yeah." Spence stared into the glass of Scotch. "This stuff tastes like medicine. Maybe worse."

"Uh-huh. I like a smooth whiskey myself."

"How come you're not home with Claire and Lucy?"

"Joe called and said he thought you might need a ride home. You seemed a bit under the weather tonight."

"The bartender?" Spence stared across the room at the man behind the bar.

"Nice guy," Johnny commented. His mouth kicked up at the corners as he studied the contents of his glass.

"Yeah." Spence wondered what his friend found so amusing in a glass of whiskey.

"I don't think you should give up on Ally."

Spence gazed at the ice cubes in his own glass. "I've sworn off women for good. Romance doesn't work for me. Never has. Never will."

"Hmm," Johnny murmured.

"How did you get Claire to agree to marriage?

You had some ups and downs. Of course there was Lucy.''

"Kids can be a great draw," Johnny admitted. "Women go all soft and tender when kids are involved."

"Yeah?" Spence perked up for a minute, then slumped in the chair. "Not Ally. Besides, she already has the twins. I have to sneak over to see 'em. Mom's the only one who will let me in the house."

"Maybe you should use a more romantic approach. Women like that."

Spence thought this through. "You think I should send her some flowers? Or maybe a box of candy. You think that would work?"

"Maybe. I was thinking more on telling Ally how you feel and how much you want a life with her. And the twins."

Spence nodded. "Yeah." He shook his head. "Nah. She knows how I feel. She always has. Did I tell you we were once best friends? Then I let sex come into it."

Johnny choked on a swallow of whisky. Spence obligingly pounded him on the back.

"But there was just the one night," he went on, "not counting graduation night, 'cause nothing happened then. We didn't, you know, go all the way."

He looked to see if Johnny was following his meaning.

His partner was having trouble with his drink. He was making some strange noises. Spence worried about him.

"Maybe you ought to change to beer," he suggested.

"Maybe."

"Anyway, that one night was the best, the very best. It was for her, too. Only it didn't take care of the hunger. You know?"

Johnny nodded, made a funny face and swallowed with an audible gulp. "Hey, Joe, how about a glass of water?"

"Sure, and the drink's too strong for a wee lad such as yourself, eh?" Joe called back. He filled a glass and brought it over to the table.

"I'll have another Scotch," Spence said.

"We'd better have coffee," Johnny told him. "Else I'll have to drive you home, then hike back for my car, then Claire will be upset. Women hate men to be late."

"Oh, yeah." Spence knew about women. They got mad for no reason that he could tell. Even his mom was irritated with him. She'd called him a dummy. "Ally called me a stupid lunkhead in front of everyone."

Johnny nodded gravely.

"So did Claire."

"She merely agreed with Ally."

"I think you did, too." Spence squinted his eyes and tried to remember. The events of the dance two weeks ago were a little confusing.

"No, that was the sheriff."

Spence snorted in disgust. "He hangs around at Ally's place all the time. Another sucker for her charm. Gary's moonstruck, too."

"Love does things like that to a man."

"Right. Well, not me." He sighed. "I wish I knew what she wanted."

Spence began to think Johnny had a serious drinking problem as he choked for the third time, this time on the water. His partner was usually controlled and as smooth as warm buttered rum. They drank coffee and talked for an hour. He realized his head hurt. Hell of a time to get a hangover. He hadn't even gotten good and smashed.

"I guess it's time to go home," Spence said. "Bed is starting to look good to me."

"You want to come over and have dinner with me and Claire?"

"I'm not good company tonight, but thanks." He walked outside with his partner, then stopped on the corner. "Johnny?"

"Yeah?"

"I think I'm going to have to leave Buttonwood, go back to Durango. I can't...I don't think I can stay here."

Johnny was silent for a minute. "Think it over, old son. Tomorrow may be a brighter day."

But Spence knew it wouldn't. Ally had rejected him. He had to leave, just as he'd done when she'd gotten engaged and married his brother.

"Your eyes look puffy again," Taylor said, casting Ally a concerned glance.

It was Monday, and they'd had lunch at the office together and were now caring for the twins.

Ally nodded. "They're like this nearly every

morning. Allergies.'' She finished changing Nick, gave him a kiss on the neck and put him down on the pallet with Taylor. Taylor handed Hannah over.

Ally changed the baby, then made funny faces at her while Taylor did the same with Nick. The twins drooled and grinned and made gleeful noises.

Both babies slept most of the night now. They had finally, as Claire had assured her would happen, gotten their days and nights straightened out.

She felt especially rested today. Rose had come over on the weekend and insisted on staying Friday and Saturday nights while Ally slept. Last night, she'd fed the babies at ten, and they'd slept until almost six this morning.

Once more, she felt she had her life under control and in good order. Except for a couple of nagging problems.

Spence was one of them. No, not him. It was the dreams he'd awakened when he'd mentioned marriage. He was merely being his noble self, taking in those who needed his care.

She was the one who'd jumped to conclusions. That he'd realized he loved her. That he couldn't live without her. That they were meant to be....

Then she'd realized they had all been caught up in the moment and the drama between Rachel and Colt, who were now married. Her eyes misted over.

Rachel had called and told her how happy she was. Colt hovered over her at the clinic, afraid the nurse was overdoing it. Rachel planned to work right up until she had to grab one of the birthing beds for herself. She and Claire and Taylor were

planning a combined bridal and baby shower for the couple next weekend.

"Ally?"

Ally abandoned her introspection at the sound of her name. "Yes?"

"I had trouble with swelling," Taylor said. "During my pregnancy."

"You were expecting twins," Ally said.

Taylor stared at her.

Slowly, the truth dawned on Ally. "You think I could be...that I might be... Oh, no, that's impossible."

"Oh." Taylor's face fell. "I'd heard...it was nothing—a rumor, that's all."

"What?" Ally demanded.

"That you and Spence McBride, well, his car was seen at your house over the weekend. I heard he'd stayed there before. In a tent, though." The college student cast a confused, apologetic glance her way.

Ally swallowed convulsively. Spence had been at her house. Over the weekend. She'd thought she'd only imagined his voice in her dreams, and the scent of his aftershave yesterday morning when she awoke.

Rose. Had she invited her son over while Ally slept?

Heat flushed Ally from head to toe. This was just too much! First he'd embarrassed her by camping out in her backyard. Then he'd humiliated her at the community park with the stupid idea about marriage. Now he'd further destroyed her reputation by

sneaking over to her house while she was inno-cently sleeping. She was just mortified!

However, she managed to joke about the situa-tion with Taylor and assure the girl there was noth-ing clandestine about her relationship with Spence. Even if Rose, whom she'd trusted, was trying to push them together.

Shocked, Ally thought about this after Taylor left for her afternoon classes. Her mother-in-law did seem to sing Spence's praises as husband-and-father material every chance she got. Ally knew Rose wanted her younger son to marry and have a family. But...with *her?*

She put the twins back in the playpen in the file room when they nodded off to sleep. It was nearly time for her afternoon appointments. She flexed her ankles. They were stiff and yes, somewhat swollen.

She thought of Taylor's embarrassed conclusion. Could she be pregnant? No, it was impossible. But if by some miracle she was...

Joy, disbelief, elation—and fear—ran through her at regular intervals, like wooden ducks lined up at a carnival. Logic shot each one down. It popped right back up.

If she was expecting, she'd have to tell Spence right away. It was what she would have told her patients. A woman had to be fair and up-front with the father. Perhaps she should pick up one of those pregnancy kits next time she was at the drugstore.

The secretary knocked, then opened the door for the first client of the afternoon. For the next few

hours, Ally put her own cares aside and listened to her patients.

At five, she packed up the twins and left the office. She went to the grocery store and did some shopping, then stopped by the pharmacy before driving home. She could see herself explaining her condition to Spence if she was pregnant.

Oh, heavens, it was too outlandish to contemplate.

"How's it going?" Spence asked Gary, getting out of his car and approaching the boy. "I saw the coach the other day. He said you were planning on trying out for football this year."

"Yeah. I was thinking of a football scholarship to college, like you had."

"You look like a runner. We could toss the ball around a bit, if you'd like, and practice some strategy."

Ally came to the back door. She looked beautiful. Her thick blond hair defiantly strayed from the band at the back of her neck. Her eyes were as blue as the sea and as deeply mysterious. He fought the tumult of feeling that seeing her produced.

He glanced at the yard. Gary had everything around the place in spit-shine condition. His mom had mentioned Ally worried about the youngster doing too much.

The twins adored the teenager. When Spence had sneaked over, the two of them had entertained the twins while Ally caught up on her sleep. So that was working out.

Over the past two weeks, he'd accepted the fact that Ally didn't really need or want him. There was passion, but it obviously wasn't enough. He hadn't a clue what was.

He heard her sigh. He glanced at her. Her eyes delved right into that secret place inside where painful things happened when he was near her. She looked away, refusing to hold his gaze for more than a second.

"The yard looks really good," he said, knowing he'd lost his best friend forever. It was time to move on. He'd spoken to the partners in his old law office in Durango during the week. They would be glad to have him back.

Gary spoke up. "Thanks. We planted bulbs all around the house and drive last weekend, and wildflowers in the meadow. There'll be hundreds of blooms next spring."

"I think Gary is going to be a horticulturist," she said, joining the conversation.

"I had a hard time deciding between law and being a fry cook," Spence told them, reaching hard for a light tone. "There was this cute redhead that worked at the fast-food place on campus. I wanted to make some points with her, but alas, she ignored my efforts to impress her."

Ally laughed along with Gary. The twins, visible on an activity pad on the floor, made joyful noises, too. "What brings you out this way?" she asked warily.

"I need to speak to you about some legal matters concerning the twins," he told her.

"Oh. Fine." She hesitated as if unsure. "We're about to eat. Would you like to join us? It's just meat loaf."

One last meal? "That would be nice," he said, his manner as formal as hers.

They were all silent as they trooped inside. The meal was delicious. Ally had learned to cook from his mother, so the food was familiar and satisfying. A vast emptiness echoed inside him at the thought. Leaving was going to be harder this time.

Harder? Looking at the little family gathered in the kitchen, he realized it was going to tear his soul apart.

When Ally finished eating, she heated the twins' formula and handed a bottle to Gary. Spence held his hand out for the other one. She gave it to him. He picked up Hannah and, talking softly, proceeded to feed the baby.

Looking at the two males, each caring for a child, her heart constricted into a tight ball of love and pain. All of them, the men and the babies, were so precious to her.

Fighting tears, she quickly ran the dishwater and washed up their dishes, leaving them to air-dry. In thirty minutes, all the chores were done. Gary prepared to go to his room over the garage.

"Dinner was really good," he said politely. He hesitated, his eyes on Spence, who was holding Hannah.

"How about I come over tomorrow?" Spence

said. "I'll bring a couple of footballs. We'll practice for an hour or so before dark."

Gary grinned and nodded.

"Hero worship," she said when he had loped out
and across the lawn. "It's good of you to take an
interest in him. He's had such a hard life."

"Gary's okay," Spence admitted. "I was wrong
about him being here."

She was surprised and touched at his admission.
"It takes so little to win the love of a child. They
want so much to please and be loved."

"Yes."

He looked at her so intently she grew flustered.
After replenishing their glasses of iced tea, she settled on the mat with Nick on her lap and played
patty-cake with him. Spence entertained Hannah.
When both babies were ready for quiet time, they
laid them on the mat.

"I have some news," he said when they were
seated opposite each other at the table.

She drew a deep breath, feeling instinctively that
she wasn't going to like hearing it. "Oh?"

"I'm going to be leaving at the end of August,"
he said softly, his strong, skillful fingers making
designs in the frost on the glass.

"Leaving?" The word made no sense.

"I'm going back to Durango. To my old office.
I'll continue to work here two days a week until I
get my court cases done and can turn over the rest
of my clients to Johnny. We're looking for someone
else to come in with him."

Her world stopped. She felt the lurch as it re-

sumed its progress through the vastness of space. The stars blinked out, one by one. The darkness closed in.

She gripped the edge of the table, realizing she was close to fainting, a thing she'd never done.

"Why?" Her voice was a whisper.

His hand tightened into a fist. He looked as if he'd like to hit something. "I'm not…happy here." He released the fist and shrugged. "I've made Nick and Hannah my heirs and am setting up trust funds for them."

She nodded as if she understood. The last star blinked out. She forced herself to breathe deeply and calmly, the way she and Taylor had learned in Lamaze classes.

She couldn't faint. She couldn't, she repeated over and over. At last her mind cleared. She faced reality.

Spence was leaving. This time he wouldn't be back. She knew it all the way to her soul. She forced back the protest that rose in her. Before she could think of another word to say, the front window exploded in a shower of glass.

Chapter Thirteen

Before Ally could react, Spence grabbed the babies, bundling them together in the mat, thrusting it into her arms and pushing all of them into the walk-in pantry. He closed the door in her face and sprinted away.

"Spence, be careful," she called, opening the door in time to see him disappear out the back exit.

"Stay inside," he called over his shoulder. The door slammed behind him.

She made a space and spread the mat on the floor. The twins were in the third state of wakefulness: crying.

"There, there," she soothed, patting them on their tummies. She stuck a finger in each gaping mouth. The babies latched on, seeking comfort after

their fright. ''Poor darlings, you've never been startled like that, have you?''

Twin pairs of blue eyes gazed solemnly at her,
their lashes wet with tears. She smiled reassuringly.
Hannah kept sucking, but Nick gave her a wobbly
smile in return. Her heart contracted with love and
pain and a thousand other emotions too deep to
name.

She heard sounds from outside, then recognized
Hank Wright's voice. She heard Spence and Gary,
too. And there were others present.

''You can't hold me. I didn't do nothing.'' The
speaker added several choice descriptive words for
the sheriff.

The person was male, probably young, certainly
defensive. A tough kid who had grown up in a
rough world. She had a feeling she knew who had
thrown the rock.

She took the twins to their new quarters and
tucked each into a crib. Gary and Hank had finished
putting the second bed together and had helped her
get the furniture into the bedrooms. Hank had put
up rods so she could hang the curtains.

Rose had brought housewarming gifts in the form
of two lamps shaped like clowns holding bundles
of colorful balloons. The clown-face clocks on the
wall in each room had been from Spence.

Flicking off the light, she hurried to the back
door. ''What's going on?''

Hank flashed her a grin in the deepening twilight.
''Caught your rock thrower,'' he told her, ''thanks

to Gary here. He alerted me there might be trouble.''

The lawman, Gary and Spence trooped into the house while a police cruiser headed out the drive toward town.

''How did you know?'' she asked the teenager while she prepared glasses of iced tea and set out a plate of cookies Rose had brought over.

Gary's expression was forlorn. His shoulders were hunched as if he was withdrawing into himself. She hadn't seen him like this since he came to live there.

''Ram's been hitting up on me since I moved here.''

She glanced at Spence, but there wasn't a trace of ''I told you so'' in his gaze. ''Did he want to move in, too?'' she asked. She'd wondered if his gang would pull something like that. With Hank and Spence around fairly often, though, she'd thought Gary was safe.

''No, he wanted me to help him rob the place. He was...he threatened to hurt...you and the twins.'' The teenager shot her a pleading glance, then stared at the floor. ''I couldn't let him do that.''

''So Gary called and told me what was going on,'' Hank added. ''Smart fella,'' he complimented the youngster.

Spence spoke up. ''Ram was trying to force Gary into agreeing to help by throwing the rocks. He thought that would frighten Gary into doing what he said.''

Ally thought of all the youngster had gone through in his life. Deeply touched, she went to Gary and, throwing her arms around him, she gave him a hard hug and a kiss on the cheek. "Thank you for caring," she whispered. "You're a wonderful person."

His face flushed and his eyes gleamed as he ducked his head. "It wasn't anything. I mean, anyone would have done it."

"Not anyone," Spence corrected. He touched the boy on the shoulder. "It takes courage to stick by your guns. Lots of people would have caved. You did the right thing."

Gary gave Spence a glance that was filled with hero worship. The praise from the two men clearly meant a lot to the teenager.

They sat around the table and discussed the culprit and gangs in general, then Hank declared he had a report to file on the incident and had better get with it. He asked if he was going to get a hug and kiss, too.

"Sure," Spence said sardonically. "Pucker up."

Hank laughed uproariously, then grabbed Ally by the shoulders. "Here's the one I meant."

Ally obligingly gave him a hug and a peck on the cheek.

"That'll do for starters," the lawman teased, "but I'll expect better…when we're alone."

"Huh," was Spence's comment on that.

With a wink at Ally and a knowing twinkle in his eyes, Hank took his leave. Gary stood, too. "I got some studying to do." He paused. "Plants are

pretty interesting. I've been thinking about studying horticulture like you said.''

"Do it only if it's your dream," Ally said, walking to the door with him, feeling that all dreams were precious and fragile and in need of nurture. "As someone once said—'This above all else; unto thine own self be true.' It's good advice."

"Shakespeare," Spence said when the youth was gone. "I remember it from senior English. We had the class together."

"Yes."

"The babies asleep?"

She listened to the monitor. "It seems so."

"Sorry I frightened them. And you. I wanted to get all of you out of harm's way."

"You caught the rock thrower." She smiled in understanding and experienced a painful onrush of tenderness for him, this friend from her childhood days. Why couldn't friendship and dreams last forever?

"Actually, Hank did."

He followed her into the living room and helped her sweep up the glass. He taped a piece of cardboard cut from a box over the opening.

"Well, that's that," she said when they returned to the kitchen. "Thanks for your help."

He crossed the room, stopping a foot in front of her, his gaze roaming her face as if looking for answers to questions only he knew. She braced herself.

"Yeah, that's that," he said. "I guess I'd better go."

She nodded. "Spence," she said, not sure what she was going to say.

"Yeah?"

"Is it because I refused your offer of marriage? Is that why you're leaving?"

His face set as if carved in stone, but his eyes...surely she'd imagined the bleakness that she had glimpsed in those dark depths.

"You were wise not to agree. I'll probably make a lousy husband." His smile was sardonic.

She thought it was also sad. "If you want marriage for the children's sake, then..." she took a deep breath "...I think I do, too."

He peered sharply at her.

She hurried on. "It can work. We have lots of things going for us. The babies. Rose. Friendship. Passion. Those could be enough."

And she would learn to live with her love for him. It would be her secret. Someday they might realize they shared more than friendship. Someday.

"It's too late, Ally. I was crazy to think I could live with that—" He broke off abruptly and pressed his finger and thumb across the bridge of his nose as if he had a headache.

"I understand," she quickly assured him.

"I have to leave, but I want a place in the twins' lives. If you'll let me see them."

"Of course." She locked her hands together to stop their trembling. "Of course you'll have a place in the twins' lives, and our—"

She stopped, horrified at what she'd nearly given away. She couldn't say anything yet. Not until she

was sure. Not until she knew what she was going to do.

"Our?" he questioned, looking puzzled. His eyes narrowed. He tilted his head slightly to the side, suspicion in his eyes. "Our what?" he asked softly, dangerously.

"Nothing. It's nothing."

He stood. She stood, too, poised either for flight or verbal combat, she wasn't sure which. She was afraid his sharp legal mind had already made the connection between her words, well before she was ready, emotionally or mentally, to cope with a new situation between them.

Misery settled like a dark cape around her shoulders. How did one tell a man intent on getting away that there was another complication, one more serious than any they had yet faced?

Spence will make a wonderful father.

He would. Ally knew that. Spence, with his big heart, his way of taking in strays and other unwanted creatures...

She drew a sharp, shaky breath. Her child would never be unwanted, would never feel the pain of rejection, of being a duty. Never!

"Ally," Spence began as the silence drew out between them. He ran a hand through his hair in obvious frustration, then laughed ruefully. "I don't want to quarrel. It's the last thing on my mind. But I have a right to know. Are you pregnant?"

The question was direct and to the point. There was a different light gleaming in his eye, but she couldn't tell how he felt.

"I'm not sure," she said. She flashed him a glance of apology for what she was about to say. "I bought one of those kits. It was positive." She stared at him helplessly. "I thought I was barren. Jack said he was okay, that the fault had to be mine. I assumed he was right, that he had checked."

Spence muttered a curse. He gestured for her to go on when she paused.

She tried to make leaving easy for him. She would rather die than have him stay out of a sense of obligation. "We can wait on making a decision. I may not be pregnant at all. It could be the tension of having the twins and...and everything."

"Everything," he repeated softly, his gaze holding hers.

His eyes reflected a lifetime of memories between them—the day she arrived with her suitcase, frightened about the future and scared to show it; school and the long, glorious days of summer; graduation night; the birth of the twins; that one night of passion that had only increased the longing.

Each memory was a separate, sharp ache in her heart, a longing for what had never been, would never be. She realized she wouldn't exchange one of those memories for a lifetime of promised happiness. Spence was woven into the very fabric of her soul.

"I'm sorry," she whispered. "It doesn't have to change your plans. You can still leave—"

"No way," he said, so fiercely she flinched. His tone softened. "I want a baby with you, maybe two, if I should be so lucky."

He took a step toward her. She stepped back. She'd spent most of her youth trying to read people, to figure out what they wanted or how she had displeased them so she could make it right. She studied Spence and tried to figure out what he was saying, what the light in his eyes meant.

But nothing made sense. Her mind refused to concentrate. The ache grew. "You're leaving," she reminded him, words so painful she could hardly get them out, but she had to. She wouldn't let him stay out of pity and responsibility.

He shook his head impatiently. "Most of all," he continued, a look of hard determination lighting his handsome face, "I simply want to be with you, every day, the two of us working together to raise this family, whether it's two kids or three. Maybe four."

Her mouth dropped open. She couldn't breathe. Her heart filled her whole chest. Spence sounded so sincere. He almost made her believe it could work.

He smiled, the saddest and most beautiful she'd ever seen. "I want my old friend back, Ally."

"You—your friend?"

"And my lover. The woman who fills my thoughts by day and my dreams by night. That's you."

"The passion," she murmured, nodding in understanding. Tears burned behind her eyes.

He frowned at her, but his tone was oddly gentle when he spoke. "More than that. It's been you from

the beginning, except I didn't realize it. And then it was too late. You were engaged to Jack.''

There was pain in his voice, in his eyes. She reached out to him, unable to bear his being hurt.

He took her hand in his. ''I played fair, Ally. I stayed away. I tried not to think of you as anything but a sister. It was hard. There were times when I knew you were unhappy.''

''How—''

''Shh,'' he said. ''You never complained, but I could see the quietness in you, the way it was when you were eleven and your dreams ended. I was careful around you and Jack. When your marriage was on shaky ground, I didn't interfere.''

With her free hand, she touched his cheek. ''Thank you for that. Neither of us could have lived with ourselves if we'd betrayed Jack or our own ideals.''

''We both made sure that was never a possibility.'' He drew a deep breath. ''But circumstances are different now. The only barriers between us that I can see are the ones we erect. I want them down. I want a life with you.''

It wasn't in his warm, caring nature to abandon his child. She had to accept that. If it broke her heart to have him but not his whole-hearted love, she would have to endure. Endurance was something she was good at.

''It might be best for the twins and the child, if there is one,'' she agreed, trying to be logical when she wanted...so many things.

Don't, she warned herself. Don't wear your heart

on your sleeve like a stray begging to be taken in. She stared out the window, afraid to meet his eyes, afraid of the tears that threatened to fall, afraid he would see the truth and feel sorry for her. Truth, she couldn't take.

To her baffled amazement, he caught her against him, wrapping his arms around her in an unyielding embrace. "All the cards, Ally. I'm playing all of mine. First, I've never met a woman I could live with. I didn't know it, but it was because of you. Because the woman had to be you."

"Oh, Spence," she whispered, stricken at the thought of his lonely years.

His gaze was hard and direct. "You were always the one. The perfect woman of my dreams whose face I could never quite see. The mate my soul searched for. My God, Ally, don't you know I love you with everything in me?"

She stared at him in confusion, unable to interpret his words or the intensity in his eyes.

He gave a groan of half despair, half ironic laughter. "I love you. I always have." His tone gentled. "I always will."

She didn't get a chance to do more than blink before his mouth plundered hers. The ground shifted under her feet. She was shaken to the depths of her being.

Spence loved her. He loved her. Spence—loved her.

A light flashed inside her, like a world exploding. It illuminated the darkest corners of her soul, free-

ing the chained hopes of her youthful heart. Spence loved her.

"Kiss me back," he demanded, his eyes going dark, almost pleading. "I need you, Ally, all of you. I'm asking for everything. You, your love, children, a lifetime."

"I do love you," she cried softly, her voice breaking.

"Thank heaven," he said fervently.

He bent to her mouth again, his passion fierce and tender and consuming. She responded just as intensely, a desert plant opening her petals to the life-giving rain of his kisses.

Her mind spun in a frantic whirl of need and disbelief and happiness...pure, unadulterated happiness.

And the tears, like a desert storm, flowed endlessly.

Spence lifted her in his arms. He settled on the living room sofa and mopped her face on his shirt. "Do you think we can be friends as well as lovers this time around?" he murmured, pressing his cheek to her hair.

"It's the best kind of relationship," she managed to assure him. "All the books say so. Husbands and wives who make it as a couple are lovers and best friends."

"Really?" he asked earnestly.

He gazed down into her face, his eyes filled with the most tender emotion she'd ever seen in him. And a little of the delightful wickedness that meant he was leading her down the garden path like the

time he'd encouraged her to pick the apples from their mean neighbor's tree.

"Then," he continued, "since we've been friends for about twenty-one years, our marriage should last even longer than that, don't you think?"

She considered, trying to subdue the tears that continued to flow, fed by a spring of inner joy, even as laughter bubbled in her. "I always know to be careful when you start asking roundabout questions that sound perfectly logical. It means I'm about to get in trouble. Like the time you talked me into picking Mrs. Snell's apples."

"Okay, just one question." His manner became serious. "Will you marry me?"

The answer came from her heart. "Yes," she said, just as solemn. "I've loved you all my life."

Pain flashed over his face. "Why didn't we say all this years ago? It's been a hell of a long time coming."

"We had a journey to make. Each of us had to make it alone, I think."

"But no more." He took her face between his hands. "No more, Ally. The future is ours, one we'll face together. Promise."

"Promise," she whispered. "Kiss me, Spence, and tell me I'm not dreaming."

He gazed deeply into her eyes. "If it's a dream, we're having the same one. A quiet wedding?"

She nodded.

"Soon?"

"Tomorrow. I don't want to wait."

"A gal after my own heart."

He stood and pulled her up. Dropping an arm over her shoulder, he led the way down the hall. "Invite me to spend the night," he urged, his voice dropping huskily and causing shivers to chase down her spine.

"You're invited." She wrapped her arms around his waist. "As if I'd let you get out of the house."

"I love a forceful woman."

Along with the humor, she felt the passion between them, a golden arc of need laced with the most intense love she could ever imagine. She had no need to hide it. He shared it, too. And that was the most miraculous thing of all.

They looked in on the sleeping babies, then went into the bedroom that would be theirs from that moment on. When they were undressed and in bed, Spence held her against him, their bodies touching in sweet intimacy. The specialness of the moment surrounded them.

They kissed, a long, deep kiss of love and promise and dreams, his and hers. They made love, fast the first time, then in a spirit of loving exploration the second time. It was, quite simply, wonderful.

Ally sat up in alarm. She stared at the window. The sun was up. Spence slept peacefully beside her, his leg touching hers, one hand tangled in her gown.

"What is it?" he asked, giving her a drowsy smile.

"The twins. It's late. They've never slept this long."

He rose with her and pulled on his pants as they

headed down the hall. Both cribs were empty. As one, they rushed to the kitchen.

"Good morning, sleepyheads," Rose greeted them with a bright smile. "My, you did sleep late. It's past nine. I called your office, Spence, right after I called the clinic and told them I wouldn't be in this morning."

Ally felt the flush start at her chest and rise in a tidal wave right up to her hairline. She went to Nick, who waited his turn for a feeding while Rose cared for Hannah.

Spence was more sanguine. "Hi, Mom." He poured a cup of coffee for himself and Ally. "Beautiful day, isn't it?"

He wasn't the least embarrassed that Ally could tell. She busily prepared Nick's bottle.

"Yes, it is," Rose agreed.

"Would it interest you to know that Ally and I have decided to get married? For the children's sake."

The smile left Rose's face. She frowned at Spence, then at Ally, who hid a smile. Trust Spence to get the most out of the situation.

"For the children...well, really," Rose spluttered. "You two are the most thick-skulled individuals I've ever met. You are madly in love with each other. Why don't you just admit it and get on with your lives? And the marriage." She gave each of them a good glare.

Spence chuckled at getting a rise out of her. He ambled over and gave her a kiss on the top of her head, then chucked Hannah under the chin. "That's

what we decided, too. Right after we got the glass cleaned up.''

"I saw Gary this morning. He told me what happened." Rose looked from one to the other. "You really are getting married? This isn't one of your jokes?"

"No way," he said. He set the coffee cup on the counter and opened the refrigerator. "How about some breakfast? A man has to keep his strength up when he takes on a family. I make the best breakfast sandwich—eggs, cheese, bacon, salsa, red pepper, avocado. Ah, some mushrooms. By the way, we might be having another baby," he said as an aside to his mother.

Rose gasped. "Ally?" she questioned.

Ally nodded. "It's early to say, but it could be true."

Rose looked thoroughly confused. Ally wasn't going to enlighten her that last night wasn't the very first she and Spence had shared. Then she saw she didn't have to.

"Well, well," Rose said, "all those headaches to get you together for nothing. Things were already moving along."

"My mother, the conniver," Spence complained to anyone who cared to listen. "At least your being sick is one worry I can wipe off my list."

Ally met the older woman's eyes. They smiled at each other, sharing their love for the man who was telling Nick and Hannah about how much they would enjoy one of his famous gourmet sandwiches when they were old enough.

"Not until they're twenty-one," Rose advised. "Oh, Colt and Rachel Rollins had an eight-pound boy last night. Everything went well according to Blanche Hastings and Flo Harris, although how they know beats me."

"The grapevine has lots of underground runners," Spence suggested. "Goes right to their houses."

The three of them laughed. Ally and Rose fed Nick and Hannah while Spence cooked the bacon.

Ally sighed in contentment and laid the sleeping Nick in the bassinet. She then dashed for the bathroom. Spence followed and held her head until her stomach calmed down.

"Hmm, maybe we'd better cut out the bacon until we get over this morning queasiness."

"We?" she questioned wryly. She brushed her teeth and splashed water on her face. He handed her a towel, then proceeded to dry her face off himself.

He gave her a kiss. "I'm in this with you. Every step of the way. Friends. Lovers. Parents. We'll share it all."

"Breathe deeply," Spence said. "Rest now. You're doing great." He wiped her face.

Ally looked up at him with her heart in her eyes. "So are you."

"Okay," Dr. Rollins said, "let's give it another try."

"Push," ordered Maryanne Winters in her don't-give-me-any-nonsense voice.

Spence smiled at Ally. "This is the big one." He kissed her forehead. "I love you."

"I love...you."

"Pant," he said, sliding his hands behind her in loving support. From the mirror positioned behind the doctor, they saw their child come into the world.

"A girl," Rachel said, entering the room as her husband tied off the cord. "She's beautiful."

"Like her mom," Spence said huskily. He pressed his cheek to Ally's. "Just like her mom."

Rose rushed in. "Darn that Dennis Reid. He wouldn't shut up so the meeting with the directors could be over. Oh, is the baby here?"

"Come in, Mom," Spence invited, "and meet our new girl, Shannon Rose McBride, named for her grandmothers. Rosie to those who know and love her."

Rose took pictures of everyone, assured Ally and Spence that Taylor and Gary were doing fine with the other two, then surprised everyone by bursting into tears.

"At last everything has worked out the way it was supposed to," she explained the emotion.

"And so it has," Spence said later that evening when visitors had come and gone. He could see Ally was tired.

When she drifted into sleep, he stood beside the bed, the little plastic bucket on wheels containing their daughter, also asleep, beside him. He recalled the day he'd come to the hospital a little over nine months ago and saw the twins come into the world.

It was the true beginning, he mused, of his and Ally's life together as parents and partners.

Lovers. Friends.

Yeah, it was all possible.

*   *   *   *   *

For more of Laurie Paige's magical writing and hearttugging stories, look for
CHEYENNE BRIDE, Laurie's contribution
to the newest Montana Mavericks series,
MONTANA MAVERICKS:
WED IN WHITEHORN,
on sale July 2000,
only from Silhouette!

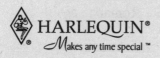

Look Who's celebrating our 20th Anniversary:

Celebrate **20** YEARS

"Let's raise a glass to Silhouette and all the great books and talented authors they've introduced over the past twenty years. May the *next* twenty be just as exciting and just as innovative!"

—*New York Times* bestselling author
Linda Lael Miller

"A visit to Silhouette is a guaranteed happy ending, a chance to touch magic for a little while.... I hope Silhouette goes on forever."

—International bestselling author
Marie Ferrarella

"Twenty years of laughter and love. It's not hard to imagine Silhouette Books celebrating twenty years of quality publishing, but it is hard to imagine a publishing world without it. Congratulations."

—International bestselling author
Emilie Richards

Silhouette®SPECIAL EDITION®

ENTER FOR A CHANCE TO WIN*

Silhouette's 20th Anniversary Contest

Tell Us Where in the World You Would Like *Your* Love To Come Alive... And We'll Send the Lucky Winner There!

Silhouette wants to take you wherever your happy ending can come true.

Here's how to enter: Tell us, in 100 words or less, where you want to go to make your love come alive!

In addition to the grand prize, there will be 200 runner-up prizes, collector's-edition book sets autographed by one of the Silhouette anniversary authors: **Nora Roberts, Diana Palmer, Linda Howard** or **Annette Broadrick**.

DON'T MISS YOUR CHANCE TO WIN! ENTER NOW! No Purchase Necessary

Where love comes alive™

Visit Silhouette at www.eHarlequin.com to enter, starting this summer.

Name:

Address:

City: State/Province:

Zip/Postal Code:

Mail to Harlequin Books: **In the U.S.**: P.O. Box 9069, Buffalo, NY 14269-9069; **In Canada**: P.O. Box 637, Fort Erie, Ontario, L4A 5X3